To Victoria

Congrats on winning my giveaway. Happy reading :-

Moonlight in
MASSACHUSETTS

THE KENNEDY BOYS BOOK ELEVEN

USA TODAY & WSJ BESTSELLING AUTHOR

SIOBHAN DAVIS

Printed by Amazon
Paperback edition © March 2022

ISBN: 9798440809352

Editor: Kelly Hartigan (XterraWeb) editing.xterraweb.com
Cover design by Robin Harper https://wickedbydesigncovers.
wixsite.com
Proofread by Bre Landers, Elizabeth Clinton and Aundi Marie.
Cover Photography by Christopher John of CJC Photography
Cover Models: Eric Taylor Guilmette and Skyler Simpson
Formatted by Ciara Turley using Vellum

An optional epilogue short novel in the highly addictive Kennedy Boys series by *USA Today* & *Wall Street Journal* bestseller Siobhan Davis.

Find out what is going on in the lives of your favorite family and their offspring. Set five years after the series end, this story begins with Selena receiving a prestigious award for Moonlight, the support center she opened to help survivors of abuse.

You can expect laughter, camaraderie, steam, a little drama and angst, and lots of love! The Kennedys are as close-knit as ever, and family still means everything to them.

This is a multiple POV short novel, including chapters from all the main characters in the series. It should be read after *Reforming Kent*.

A Note from the Author

This multiple-POV, short novel features one chapter from each of the main characters from the series. This book should only be read after *Reforming Kent*.

Some of the characters are Irish, and although they have lived in the US for many years, a lot of their dialogue and inner monologue is still Irish. We phrase things differently, so if anything seems odd, it is due to cultural differences in speech patterns and colloquialisms.

Moonlight in MASSACHUSETTS

THE KENNEDY BOYS BOOK ELEVEN

Chapter One
Selena

Nerves fire at me from all angles, but I plaster a smile on my face and look up at the MC as he begins the video introduction. Keanu slips his hand into mine and squeezes. He moves his mouth to my ear. "Breathe, baby. I've got you. You know you can do this," he says as a round of applause breaks out in the crowded ballroom of the prestigious five-star hotel. The prerecorded short video starts playing, and my muscles relax the instant I see Moonlight, my sanctuary for abuse survivors, on the screen. The opening scene is an aerial shot, and it showcases the facility in perfect clarity.

"You should be proud," Eva whispers, from the other side of me. "This is the manifestation of all your hard work and dedication. You deserve this, and your speech will be great. Try not to worry." Her sincere warm brown eyes lock on my face. "You run a multimillion-dollar charity organization that has supported thousands of survivors in the three years since you opened your doors. A little speech won't faze you."

"Thank you," I choke out over a lump in my throat. "I have gotten better at public speaking, but it's still not easy."

"You will do everyone proud, and we're here for you."

I smile as I glance along the row where our family is seated. Everyone is here. Well, the adults plus the teenagers. The younger kids are at home with babysitters, but we have a party arranged for them tomorrow when we all get together for a private family dinner at my in-laws' house.

Brad and Rachel flew in from Ireland, where they've been based these past eighteen months, and Mom cut her honeymoon short to be here. I'm touched both couples made the effort to attend. It means a lot to me. "I'm grateful to have so much support. Every day, I count my blessings to have such an amazing family."

It's no lie. I lost my biological family to the monsters who kidnapped me, and after I escaped, it was just Sandrine—my adopted mom—and me for a long time. Until I married Keanu and inherited his family. I adore the Kennedys, and they have welcomed Mom and me with open arms.

Life is pretty damn perfect. Even my inability to conceive a child these past five years didn't put a damp-ener on my mood for long. I never forget what I went through and how different things could be now, so I'm grateful for every blessing and fortunate for everything and everyone I have in my life. Perhaps that is the reason why—

"You're missing it," Keanu whispers, cutting through my thoughts as he jerks his head at the screen. I redirect my gaze to the video, smiling at Ulrich's handsome face as he talks animatedly about his time at Moonlight. I have seen this video countless times already, but a surge of pride swells my chest each time I watch it.

On the screen, I'm giving a whistle-stop tour of the facility, pausing to chat to some of our residents. A couple of them kindly agreed to provide biographies and to talk about their time at Moonlight, describing how it has helped them to process their trauma and taught them new coping strategies. The work my team does doesn't stop there though. We have a ton of programs that provide new skills and a range of ways we support their future plans in preparation for when they return to life outside the facility.

Another round of applause breaks out as the video ends, and the MC clears his throat. "Our annual awards celebrate the work of charities, community groups, individuals, and voluntary organizations who have made a difference in our society and changed our country for the better. This is an opportunity to shine a light on the unsung heroes who dedicate themselves to others. Tonight, we have recognized and celebrated many people and organizations who have been a lifeline for others through the support they provide. Once again, I would ask you to join me in thanking all of them for their efforts."

Robust applause rings out around the large elegantly decorated ballroom. When hush descends again, the MC continues while I fight a fresh bout of nerves. "Our final award of the night is the Impact Award. This award is given to one enterprise or individual who has achieved a significant impact in their charitable endeavors. A person or entity who has set a guiding light for others to follow and brought awareness to a cause. Tonight, we are delighted to present this award to Selena Kennedy and Moonlight. As we have just seen, the support services they offer to victims of sex trafficking and sexual abuse is unprecedented and beyond anything else available within the US. We believe Moonlight paves the way for other similar rehabilitative facilities, which are much needed in our society, but it is more than that. Selena herself has bravely spoken about her own experiences and in doing so has highlighted the very concerning issue of global human trafficking. Selena is spearheading a lobby group to secure more funding to support survivors and to establish a specialist sex trafficking unit to bring more heat down on these criminals. She is an inspiration to all of us and a very worthy recipient of this special award."

Raucous applause breaks out as the tall, gray-haired MC smiles and gestures for me to approach. My family and friends stand, as I rise, beaming at me with proud smiles. Mom and Alex have tears in their eyes, and if I'm not mistaken, I think Kyler has too. "I'm so proud of you, Sel." Keanu bends his head and kisses me. "You amaze me every single day."

"I love you." I give him a quick hug.

"You've got this," he reminds me, squeezing my hand.

"I do." Thrusting my shoulders back, I project confidence as I walk up the steps to the podium. I might be a basket case on the inside, but I won't let my team or the residents down. This is as much their award as it is mine.

Behind me, my family whoops and hollers and shouts out their encouragement.

The MC shakes my hand before giving me a crystal cup engraved with a personal plaque. We turn to the front, facing the crowd, as more applause rings out, and several camera flashes go off as the press in attendance takes photos. A few catcalls ring out from the front row, and I don't need to look to know it's Kalvin and Kent.

When the ruckus has died down, I place the cup on a side table and discreetly wipe my clammy palms down the sides of my figure-hugging, long, gold and silver ball-gown. Approaching the microphone, I adjust it to my height and pray I remember the words I memorized this past week. Even though reading my speech would be far easier, I want this to be from the heart.

"I would like to thank the Charity Enterprise Corporation for this amazing honor. I am humbled and awed to be recognized in this way and thrilled to be among so many incredible people here tonight who have done so much for their communities and to support others. This award means a lot to me, not just because it helps to validate the work we are doing at Moonlight, and to bring even more awareness to the services we provide, but mostly because it is the culmination of years and years of hard work by so many people to get this charity off the ground."

I gulp back my nerves. "I have a lot of people I need to thank, so please bear with me." I offer a nervous smile to the crowd before my gaze instantly finds my husband's. Keanu's encouraging smile helps to scrub the edge off my anxiety.

"Firstly, I want to thank my husband for always believing in me and helping to make this happen. From the first moment I met Keanu, as a frightened traumatized fifteen-year-old, he has sought to support me and raise me up, and his love has given me the strength and the courage to battle my demons and fight to bring awareness to the global human-trafficking problem." I look down at my husband with a heart full of love. "Moonlight would not exist without him, and I owe him so much. I love you, Keanu."

He blows me a kiss, and the last of my anxiety fades away. I return my focus center stage and continue. "I also need to thank my mother, Sandrine Douglas, for her constant kindness, love, and support. She welcomed me into her home, knowing how broken I was, and never for one minute did her support waver. She helped me to become the woman I am today, as did my therapist, Denise, a woman who gently coaxed me back to life. She couldn't be here tonight, but she is the unsung heroine in my story."

My gaze lowers to the Kennedys, and the outpouring of love and pride is almost tangible. "I owe the entire Kennedy family a debt I can never repay. Thank you, Alex, for giving me a chance when most fashion labels would not have hired a model with such limitations. Thank you for your kindness and for opening your family to me."

"We love you," my mother-in-law mouths, and I wish I could hug her, to let her know how much I appreciate her. I think she knows, and hopefully my words cement it.

Forcing my wandering mind to focus, I return to my speech. "Not only have the Kennedys made me feel loved and cherished, but every single person in my family has contributed in some way toward Moonlight. Thank you, Kalvin, for diligently working for years with a skilled team of architects to bring my vision for the facility to life."

Kalvin nods, looking a little sheepish, which is most unlike him.

"My mother-in-law and father-in-law fundraised tirelessly to get the development off the ground, and they have personally donated on an annual basis. All my brothers-in-law and their spouses have contributed in different ways. Thank you all from the bottom of my heart for giving up your precious time to give back to others. You are all wonderful people with big hearts, and I'm so blessed to call you my family."

My chest heaves with powerful emotion as I push on. "I need to say a special thanks to Kyler Kennedy. Kyler works full-time at Moonlight as our CFO, and it is his financial expertise and insight that allow us to offer so many survivors a temporary home while they heal. Kyler's passion for the work we do matches my own, and I hope you know I could not do it without you," I say, looking at my brother-in-law as he fights to hold back his tears.

My attention turns to the row behind my family, where some of our employees sit. "Moonlight has been successful because the team of people we have on our staff are some of the leading specialists in the country, if not the world. Thank you, Faye, for helping me to recruit the best because our residents deserve the best care." I smile at Kyler's wife and Keanu's cousin before my gaze skims over my employees. "Some of our team are here tonight though most could not attend as they are working. I would like to ask you all to stand, please." I direct my request to the team of fifteen staff members in the second row.

Slowly, they rise, and a new surge of pride flows through my veins. "These people, ladies and gentlemen, are the true recipients of this award. These men and women work tirelessly, day after day, giving way more than their contracted hours, because they are compassionate, selfless people who live for others." My family begins clapping as I join in, and then the whole room acknowledges my team. My heart is so full it feels like it might burst.

After the applause has died, I nod, and my staff reclaims their seats. I take a sip of my water as I prepare to bring my speech to a close. "Lastly, I want to thank every resident who has walked through the gates of Moonlight. Thank you for trusting us to help you with your healing process. Thank you for never giving up. For consistently fighting to reclaim the life that was stolen from you. Because of you, I will never stop fighting for justice for survivors of abuse. Every day, you all make me proud. You are the reason I do this, the reason I will continue to do this, and the reason I will fight tooth and nail to bring more awareness to this very serious issue. Every child deserves to have a childhood full of laughter and innocence and love. No child should have to endure the things we endured."

Wetting my lips, I look up, skimming my gaze over the audience. "The things that happened to me could have broken me permanently. I am fortunate because I had people who loved me and encouraged me to work through my pain and my feelings to find myself again. No survivor of abuse will ever be the same. The experiences we have faced transform us in ways we can't always change, but I am living proof it is possible to suffer horrific abuse and come out the other side. Changed but stronger. I want to ensure every survivor gets the opportunity to heal the way I did. At its core, that is what Moonlight is about. It's a sanctuary, a safe haven, and a place where survivors can rediscover themselves in a protective environment."

I lift the cup up beside me, resting it on the edge of the podium. "This award, and the accompanying acknowledgement, will help to ensure the work we have started gets to continue. From the bottom of my heart, and on behalf of all abuse survivors, thank you."

Chapter Two
Keanu

I thrust inside my wife, stroking her tight walls with my cock, as I leisurely glide in and out of her pussy. "I love you," I say before leaning down to kiss her. I must have told her a hundred times in the past twenty-four hours. I am so proud of her, and I don't think I have ever loved her as much as I do right now. Which says a lot, because the love I have for the woman moaning and writhing underneath me in our bed is immeasurable and never ending.

"I'm living my best life with you." Sel grabs my face and kisses me fiercely as I pick up my pace and rock into her a little harder. "And it's only getting better."

We exchange an excited smile, and I go still inside her, taking a moment to appreciate her and everything she has given me. "How did I get this lucky?" I dot soft kisses all over her face. "How is it I love you more and more every day?"

"How is it you've stopped moving?" My wife arches a brow, and I chuckle. Selena is this perfect combination of innocent angel and devilish minx. Her long white-blonde hair fans out around her on the pillow as she arches her hips, urging me to move.

"I want to memorize this moment. To add it to the others I have stored up here." I tap my temple. "I have hundreds of perfect moments captured, and I want thousands more with you."

Tears prick her eyes as her fingers move to my face, tracing over the soft stubble on my chin and cheeks. "Always so poetic. I love you for eternity, Keanu, but if you don't start moving—"

I cut her off with a passionate kiss as I finish making love to her, bringing us both over the edge quickly when I realize the time.

"The woman of the hour is finally here," Mom says, opening the door to us, a couple of hours later, when we arrive at my parents' house.

"Sorry we're a little late," I say, handing her a large bouquet of red and yellow roses.

"Thank you, sweetie, and it's fine. I know you must both be exhausted after yesterday." Mom places the flowers on the hall table behind her.

"Thank you so much for everything you have done to help me and for hosting dinner today," Selena says, looking tired but happy. It's been a busy, stressful few weeks, but she never complains. The MC was right last night. She's such an inspiration, and I'm so freaking lucky to call her mine.

Mom envelops Selena in a warm embrace. "I'm so proud of you, honey."

I chuckle because Sel must have heard that a thousand times yesterday. My family was all super emotional listening to my wife's heartfelt speech. I love how much they love her and vice versa. We may have had our moments in the past, but our family is close. There isn't anything I wouldn't do for my brothers, their spouses, or their kids, my parents too, and I know I can always count on them as well. Family is everything, and they are going to be thrilled when they hear our news—both announcements.

"Hey, Keanu. Selena," Hewson says, arriving in the grand hallway of my parents' lavish home. He's my eldest nephew, and I can't believe he turned sixteen in May. He towers over all of us except for Kaden who still has an inch on him. "Grandma, Gramps is looking for you. He can't find the champagne glasses or something."

Mom rolls her eyes. "I swear I can't leave him alone for a minute. He'd be useless without me."

"He was," I say, remembering the years my parents were separated and living in different houses. Thank God, they were able to repair their relationship and to emerge even stronger than before. "He doesn't exist well without you."

"Aw." Mom clasps my cheeks, like I'm five. "I used to think Keaton was my sweetest child, but I think you've claimed the crown."

"He can keep it," I say, winking at Hewson as I sling

my arm around my wife's shoulders. "No man in his thirties likes to be called sweet."

"Or a child," Hewson adds, looping his arm through Mom's and giving her a pointed look. I know my nephew thinks he's a man because he sure as fuck looks like one and he's sixteen, an age when most teen boys are at their cockiest. Most of us were. The truth is, you have got no clue at sixteen. Hewson is at that in-between stage—a kid becoming a man, one who is trying to figure out his place in the world. He's a good kid, even if Kal and Lana are dealing with teenage hormones and a sizable attitude. Apart from partying—which none of us can criticize seeing as we were doing the exact same at his age—he hasn't caused them any trouble.

It could be a lot worse.

"I don't want you to grow up." Mom pouts, smushing his cheeks together. "You are all growing up too fast. Slow down." She tweaks his nose before pressing a kiss to his cheek.

Mom adores her grandchildren, all fourteen of them. Sixteen, if you count Rachel and Brad's two, which Mom does. But Hewson occupies a special place in her heart because he was the first. Not that she'd ever admit that. Mom wouldn't want any of the kids to feel any more or less special, but I can tell.

We trail Mom and Hewson into the main living space where the rest of our family is waiting, minus the younger kids, who must either be outside at the playground or in the game room. Mom hired an entertainer, and Kyler and Faye's part-time nanny, Samantha, is here to keep the kids occupied so the adults can talk for a change. Usually, when we all get together, we only manage to grab snatched conversations.

We make our hellos and accept a glass of champagne from Dad. "A toast," he says when all the adults have a flute. "To Selena and Moonlight. Congrats, honey. We're all so proud of you."

Everyone offers their congrats, and we chink glasses.

"You gave a beautiful speech, darling," Sandrine says, wrapping her arms around her daughter. "I know you still hate public speaking, but you were a complete pro. It was perfect."

"Thanks, Mom." Selena extracts herself from Sandrine's arms to give her stepdad, Paul, a quick hug. "Thank you both for cutting your honeymoon short to attend. I didn't expect that, but it wouldn't have been the same without you."

It's such a shame Denise couldn't be there. She had a stroke last year, which left her paralyzed from the neck down. She lives full-time in a retirement home, and we visit her weekly. Her mind is still sharp even if her body has let her down. Cheryl recorded Selena's speech, and she has already emailed us a copy so we can show it to Denise at our next visit.

"We wouldn't have missed it for the world," Paul says, reaching down to grasp his wife's hand.

Sandrine surprised us all a year ago when she announced she was in a relationship with a man fifteen years younger than her. Paul is a junior partner at Stearns & Westfall, the law firm Kent works at. It was a whirl-wind romance, but the two have known each other for years through their work in the legal system. Sandrine has presided over several of Paul's cases in court. They got engaged three months ago and wed in a small ceremony ten days ago at city hall. Selena is delighted for her mom. I know she worried about her living alone.

"Congratulations on your marriage," Kent says, coming up beside us. "I didn't get a chance to talk to you last night before you left." The party lasted into the small hours of the morning, but Sandrine and Paul had left shortly after Selena received her award, citing jet lag.

"Thank you," Paul says. "Congrats on your promotion. It's very well deserved." Kent passed the bar a couple of years ago, and he was recently appointed to a senior attorney position at the firm he has worked for since he graduated law school. He likes it there, and he has garnered quite the reputation as an advocate of children's rights.

Kent's seven-year-old daughter Shania is clinging to his back like a spider monkey, her small hands wrapped around her dad's throat.

"Where's your partner in crime?" I ask, looking around for Austen and Keaton's son because those two are joined at the hip and one is never far from the other.

"My what?" Shania asks, her brow puckering.

"Eliot," Selena clarifies, reaching her arms out for the little girl.

Emotion swirls through my veins as my wife lifts Shania off Kent's back, placing her feet on the ground, and Shania throws herself at Sel, hugging her. "We had a fight. He's a stupid boy," she says, sniffling a little. "All boys are stupid."

"They are," Kent agrees, crouching down in front of

his only child. "It would be fantastic if that sentiment could be imprinted in your brain for the next thirty years or more."

Shania's nose scrunches in confusion.

"But Eliot is your cousin and your best friend, and you were really looking forward to playing with him at the party." He unfurls to his full height, taking his daughter's hand in his. "Let's go find him so you two can make up."

"I think we have the same idea," Austen says, entering the room from the hallway. "We were just coming to find the princess," he adds, bending down in front of his son. "Don't you have something to say to Shania, Eliot?"

Keats steps into the living room, carrying his sleepy-eyed three-year-old daughter in his arms. Austen straightens up as Eliot walks toward Shania.

"I'm sorry for pulling your hair," Eliot says, his lower lip wobbling as he looks at Shania. "I just got mad when you said Taylor was better than me at Little League."

"Oh boy." Kent smothers a chuckle as Keats's lips curve at the corners. He gently rocks Lia as Austen puts his palm on the top of her head.

The kids are competitive, and it's clear the Kennedy blood flows through their veins. We used to argue like crazy over sports and games growing up, and it's amusing to see the next generation is as spirited as we were.

Selena slinks up alongside me, and I tuck her into my side, holding her close as we watch the drama unfold. Our eyes meet, and I see the same expectation on her face as I'm feeling. I'm bursting to tell everyone our news.

"Well, duh." Shania rolls her eyes at Eliot. "I only said that to cheer Taylor up because Cathal said Taylor throws like a girl. Everyone knows you're the shit at baseball."

"You're not supposed to say shit," Eliot replies. "My dad says it's a bad word." Dad means Austen, because Keaton is Daddy to their kids.

"Well, my daddy tells my mommy she's the shit in bed." Shania bats her long eyelashes at Kent. "It's okay if you say it. Right, Daddy?"

"Presley will rip you a new one if she hears about this," I mutter to my triplet while we all try not to laugh.

"You need to stop eavesdropping on adult conversation," Kent says, fighting a smirk. "What do you say to Eliot?"

"You're forgiven." Shania throws her arms around Eliot, and he hugs her to his chest. Though they are roughly the same age, he's a good head taller than his cousin. His eyes close as he hugs her, and she seems to melt into him. It's super cute.

"I think we might have a future Kyler and Faye in the making," Selena says.

"Nope." Kent shakes his head. "Do not start that shit, Sel."

"Dinner's ready!" Mom hollers, and we all traipse into the dining room. Mom got rid of the formal living room a few years ago, knocking down the wall so she could enlarge the dining space to accommodate her expanding family. We always use the larger, more casual living room anyway, so it was a good call.

It's sheer bedlam getting sixteen kids and twenty

adults seated for dinner, even if Mom had two long tables custom made to fit us all and she brought caterers in today, but eventually we manage it.

After dinner, the kids disappear to the game room while the adults enjoy a more leisurely dessert. The women are drinking wine while the guys drink beer. Sel sips a mineral water, which isn't unusual. My wife isn't a big drinker. We are all staying over tonight, which is something we haven't done in a long time.

"Faye tells me you two are thinking about adopting a teenager?" Rachel says, her gaze bouncing between me and my wife.

I nod. "It's more than just thinking about it. We began the process a few months ago, and we sign the paperwork to adopt Jett in three weeks."

"That's great news," Brad says, resting his arm along the back of his wife's chair.

"I'm happy for you guys," Rachel says. "There are so many kids who need a good home. You will make great parents."

"I couldn't agree more," Selena says, looking at me with dancing eyes.

"I'm pleased it worked out," Keven says, leaning his elbows on the table. "I had a feeling when I was sending Jett your way that this kid was special."

"He was sex trafficked?" Rachel asks in a low tone.

Selena nods. "His family was attacked while they were on vacation in Mexico. He was taken and sold. His family was found burned in their car. It was staged to look like an accident."

"No one knew Jett was missing," Keven continues

explaining, "because there were no IDs on the family. By the time the maternal grandparents came forward, Jett was long gone. We found him a year later when we busted this ring in a joint mission with the Mexican authorities. Poor kid was in a bad way. There was something about him that made me take a special interest. I looked him up a year later. He was living with his grandparents, but they couldn't handle him. They are old, and he was out of control. I knew I had to do something. If I left him there, he would turn to a life of crime or end up hurting himself, so I called Selena, and she took him in."

"He reminds me a lot of myself," Sel quietly says. "He rarely speaks, and he's very withdrawn. He flinches from touch. He has made progress in the months he's been at Moonlight, but he still has a long way to go." She looks up at me with tears in her eyes. "When we couldn't conceive, we agreed to adopt, but we hadn't planned on taking in a teenager until we met Jett."

We have spent five years trying to have a baby. Attending specialist visit after specialist visit when nothing happened month after month. We discovered there is some damage to Selena's uterus from the abuse she suffered as a young child. The doctors said we could still conceive but it would be difficult.

"No one wants to adopt teens," Lana says. "I conducted research for a book I'm writing, and I spoke to an adoption agency recently. They said everyone wants babies, and couples are reluctant to adopt teens, especially troubled teens. I think what you are doing is wonderful. Jett is lucky he crossed paths with you when he did."

"I'm sorry you weren't able to have a baby of your own, Selena. I know how much you both wanted that," Sandrine says, "but I speak from experience when I say adopting a child is one of the most incredible things a person can do." She plants a hand over her chest. "What I feel in here is no less than what I would feel if I'd had a biological child. I love you as much as I would have if I'd given birth to you myself. You two have an infinite supply of love to give, and I know you will love that boy as if he is your own flesh and blood."

"Thanks, Mom. And I love you too." Selena gets up and hugs her mother, and it's a tender moment. Mom clasps my hand. I know she gets all emotional seeing how freely Selena shows her love now. There were many years where she couldn't handle touch, and we had to be careful not to overstep a line and trigger her anxiety. Watching her doing something simple as hugging her mother is magical because it highlights how far she has come and how hard she fought to truly live.

I hope one day we can be that for Jett.

Selena looks up at me, nodding and smiling. "We actually have more good news to share," I say, standing as Selena comes back around to me. I pull her to my front and wrap my arms around her. "The week after we began the adoption process, we discovered Selena is pregnant."

There are two seconds of shocked silence, and then everyone erupts, jumping up to come and hug us and offer their congratulations. Both our moms are crying. "Oh, honey." My mom envelops us both in a hug, pressing a kiss to our brows. "This is the best news ever. I'm so happy for you."

"We've gone from a family of two to a family of four practically overnight, and we couldn't be happier."

"It's wonderful you are still going ahead with the adoption," Mom says. "I can't wait to meet both my new grandchildren."

"Absolutely," Sel replies. "We made a commitment to Jett, and us having a baby doesn't change that."

"How far along are you?" Cheryl asks.

"We had our sixteen-week ultrasound during the week," I say. "We were bursting to tell everyone, but we wanted to wait until we were sure everything was okay."

"That's understandable," Eva says. "Do you know if you're having a boy or a girl?"

Selena looks up at me, asking a silent question.

"It's your call, baby," I say.

"We're having a little girl," Sel exclaims, her cheeks bright with excitement as she retrieves the ultrasound photo from her purse. My sisters-in-law crowd around, oohing and aahing over it.

"How precious." Mom leans into Dad, snuggling into his side, and her delight is obvious to see.

"Congrats, son." Dad squeezes my shoulder. "I'm made up for you."

I grin, loving how his Irishness creeps into the conversation every now and then. "Thanks, Dad."

"You're going to have your hands full with a demanding baby and a moody teen," Kalvin says, grabbing me into a man hug. "But there is no better man for the job. You're going to make wonderful parents. I'm so happy for you, little brother."

"Thanks, man."

"You might be able to coax Hewson into babysitting if you throw him some clothes."

My fashion brand recently added a young adult line to our collection, and my nephew has been dropping hints the past couple of times I met him.

"I'll babysit anytime," Hewson instantly offers from his seat at the table. I thought he had disappeared with Matthew to play video games, but he must have come back without me noticing.

"Clothes in exchange for babysitting. We can do that," I reply. "I was actually planning to ask if you had any interest in modeling for me?"

Hewson almost chokes on his soda. His wide blue eyes pin mine in place. "Is this a joke?"

I chuckle at the horrified look on his face. "It's a serious offer."

"I think you'd make a great model," Faye says, failing to hide her grin.

"Thanks, but no thanks. Babysitting I can do. I draw the line at modeling."

"Pity," Sel says. "You have amazing cheekbones, and with your height and build, I bet you'd be a natural."

"I'll stick to the football field," Hewson replies, and I can tell he wants to end this conversation pronto.

"I wouldn't be so hasty to turn your uncle down," Kalvin says, dragging a hand through his dark hair. "Chicks dig models. You'd have girls crawling all over you."

"Stinky!" Lana yells, throwing cautionary eyes at her husband. "Do not encourage that!"

Hewson smirks, leaning back in his chair. "I have

girls crawling all over me now, and that's before I've taken my clothes off."

"Oh my God." Lana buries her head in her hands.

Mom says, "I think that's quite enough of this conversation." She eyeballs Hewson. "I hope you always use a condom."

A chorus of "Mom!" rings out, followed by loud groans.

"I think she's even more embarrassing than when we were kids," Kal says.

"That's not even remotely possible," Kyler says. "If there's one thing Mom is, it's consistently embarrassing."

Chapter Three

Lana

"**W**hy do I have to sit on a booster seat?" Heather grumbles as I strap her in the back of Kal's Lincoln Navigator. "Boosters are for babies!"

"You are five, little terror, and I hate to break it to you," Kal says, glancing over his shoulder into the back seat, "but you will be sitting on that booster for many years to come."

"Boosters aren't for babies," Hewson adds, powering up Heather's iPad. "Babies sit in baby seats, and you need to sit on a booster to keep you safe while Dad or Mom is driving." He pulls up *Beauty and the Beast*, the cartoon version, which is my youngest daughter's current obsession, and hands the iPad to her. We only have a fifteen-minute drive to our house, but Heather can't sit still for fifteen seconds without some distraction. It's way past her bedtime, but we know from experience she won't sleep on the ride home. She's a live wire who seems to exist on minimal sleep, which is why Kal and I constantly have dark shadows under our eyes. Still, I wouldn't swap her for the world. She's so energetic and vibrant, and she brings enormous enjoyment to our lives.

We had initially planned on staying the night with my in-laws and the extended family, but my husband knows me well. After we learned Selena and Keanu's amazing happy news, he knew I would want to return home.

"Hewson and I both sat on boosters until we were eleven," Hayley replies, not lifting her head from her cell phone. She's only twelve, and I held out as long as I could before giving her one, relenting when every other child had a phone. Kal has installed parental control measures, so we can screen what she's doing, which helps to assuage my fears. I don't want to breach my eldest daughter's privacy, but I need to know she's safe. There are tons of sick predators who prey on vulnerable kids, and our children are at higher risk because of the family they come from.

"Well, I hate it!" Heather proclaims, placing her headphones on her ears and plugging them into the iPad.

Hewson grins at me through the mirror as I climb into the passenger seat. Kal chuckles as he starts the engine, moving his hand to my knee, giving me a reassuring squeeze. "Never a dull moment with our little terror. Imagine how fun the teenage years are going to be."

"God help us all." I kick my shoes off as Kal maneuvers the car down the winding driveway.

It's late when we get home, and I'm yawning as I open the front door. Kal disappears with Heather. We both know he'll have more success getting her asleep quicker than me. Hewson retrieves our overnight bags from the trunk while Hayley kisses me goodnight.

"Want me to make you some herbal tea?" Hewson asks after dumping all the bags in the entryway, locking his dad's car, and shutting the front door.

"That would be lovely. Thanks, love." I stretch up as he leans down, letting me wrap my arms around him in a hug. It's not often Hewson offers hugs these days, so I'm going to milk it for as long as I can get away with this.

My son is a giant, towering over me, and he even has a few inches in height on his father. He's broader than Kal too, something he loves to tease his dad about. They work out together, either at our home gym or a local place they joined, and I love how close they are. It's been challenging the past year as Hewson battles to gain his independence and seek his place in the world. But he's still only sixteen, and he needs our guidance now more than ever.

Hewson has given us more trouble this past year than ever before.

He was always a mild-mannered, easygoing, happy kid full of childhood wonder and innocent mischief, so the regular arguments cropping up over boundaries have been most unwelcome. Kal and Hewson have butted heads a lot, and I worry one of these days something will be said that will irreparably damage the solid relationship they have. I end up acting as peacemaker, in an attempt to avoid that, when the truth is I'm as worried as Kal. I know it's his hormones, and the pressure of the society we live in, and the family he comes from. Deep down, he's a

Siobhan Davis

real good kid, but I can't help worrying. These are formative years when a large part of who he will become as a man starts taking shape.

I want to encourage and guide him, without clipping his wings, while ensuring he is safe. To me, he will be always be my little boy. The sweet cutie who sang nursery rhymes until his voice turned hoarse. The enchanted believer who gobbled up the fantasy stories I read to him each night and hoarded dinosaur toys. The exuberant adventurer who giggled and screamed when his dad chased him around the garden, playing hide and seek or cops and robbers. The affectionate son who loved snuggles with his mom and always knew how to cheer me up when I was sad.

"Is everything okay, Mom?" he asks, pressing a kiss to my cheek before breaking our embrace.

"Everything is fine," I lie. "I was just reminiscing about you as a little boy." I pat his chest. "You were the apple of my eye then, and you still are." Tears stab my eyes as a surge of unexpected emotion clogs my throat. "I hope you know how much I love you, Hewson. I know things have been a bit strained around here lately, but it's only because your father and I love you so much."

"I know that, Mom." A sigh escapes his lips. "But you've got to trust me more. It feels like you and Dad don't trust me at all."

"We do trust you." I am quick to reassure him. "It's others we don't trust."

His features soften in understanding. "I know this is coming from a good place. I know what happened to you when you were a teen, so I get it, but you and Dad have warned me a lot. I know there are people out there who will try to take advantage of me. I'm always on my guard, and I won't let that happen."

The internet is a fantastic modern invention. Technology advances at such a rapid pace, and there are so many things kids these days get to do and have access to that we didn't. I try to remember it's a positive advancement. But it's hard when the news of what I did to their father—and why—is out there for them to see, should they choose to search for it. Occasionally, some article will dredge that horrible part of our past back up, and it always sends me into a mini depression.

We chose to tell Hewson the true facts when he was twelve, and we recently spoke with Hayley too. We would rather they hear about it from us. Both our children were upset, and it took them a few days to process it all, but ultimately, they were understanding when they learned how it had all gone down.

"Good." I squeeze his hand. "I want the best life for you, Hewson. You deserve to have the world. If we set boundaries, it's because we are protecting that future for you."

"I know, Mom. I do, but you've got to let me make mistakes too. It's part of growing up. I'm pretty sure Dad and my uncles were doing far worse than me at this age."

Isn't that the truth.

I could continue protesting, but it's late, and I don't want to end the day arguing with my son. "It's late, and some of us need our beauty sleep. I'm going to read in the sunroom for a while."

"I'll make your tea and bring it to you there."

I settle into the comfy reading seat by the window of our sunroom, peering out the glass at the pitch-black night, while I contemplate life. Hewson bids me good night after bringing me my tea, and I sip from the cup as I attempt to read, but my brain won't switch off long enough for me to focus, so I give up and quietly stew.

That's how my husband finds me ten minutes later. Kal moves behind my chair, his hands landing on my shoulders as he gently kneads the tense muscles he finds there. "Talk to me, honeybun," he softly says, leaning down to kiss my neck. "Tell me what's going through your mind."

"Horrible selfish thoughts," I admit as the first tear rolls down my face.

Kalvin stops massaging my shoulders and moves in front of me, kneeling between my legs and taking my hands in his. "That's not possible. There isn't a selfish bone in your body."

Agony coats my throat, and I work hard to stifle the anguish dying to burst free from my lips.

"I hate seeing you so upset. Perhaps we should have told them. Everyone would have understood." Kal reaches up to swipe the tears from my cheeks.

"No." I vigorously shake my head, forcing myself to get a grip. I thread my fingers through my husband's, needing his touch to comfort and ground me. "Nothing should detract from Sel and Keanu's news. They tried so long to have a baby. All those disappointments must have been heartbreaking for them. This is the best news ever, and our news would have only put a dampener on things. I didn't want that for them. I know you didn't either."

"Of course not, but your feelings matter too. It's okay to be upset. It's a natural human reaction."

"I am happy for them, Stinky. I truly, genuinely am."

"I know that, sweetheart," he says, climbing to his feet. Wordlessly, he lifts me before sitting in my seat and situating me in his lap.

I rest my head on his shoulder and place my hand on his toned chest. My husband is still a total hottie, and I desire him now as much as I always have. Maybe more so as he gets older. But this isn't about lust. I need him to hold me and tell me it's going to be all right. That I'm not a monster for thinking the thoughts I'm thinking. We don't keep secrets from one another anymore, so I tell him what's going through my mind even if I'm embarrassed by what I'm thinking. "Our kids would have been born mere weeks apart, and I'm afraid their baby will always be a reminder of the baby we lost. I'm afraid I will look at Selena as her pregnancy progresses and resent her for it."

Silent tears seep from my eyes. "I don't want to resent her. She's the sweetest, kindest, most loving person, and she deserves this more than anyone I know. I want to be happy for her. For them. To help her celebrate, but how can I do that when all I will think is how that should have been me? We should be pregnant together, just like Cheryl and me were with Talisa and Heather."

"These feelings won't last forever, Lana." Kalvin cups my cheek and tilts my face up so he's looking at me. "We only lost our baby two weeks ago. We're still grieving, and it's good you are voicing these thoughts and expunging them." He looks tired as he leans in and softly kisses me. "We will get through this, and I know you'll support

Selena like you have done all our sisters-in-law, because that's the kind of woman you are. The truth is, their child will probably remind us, from time to time, of the child we lost. But we don't want to forget our little angel in heaven, and the time will come when we can speak about it without so much pain in our hearts."

"Do you really believe that?" I sniffle, pressing my face into his warm neck. The scent of his citrusy cologne is a welcome balm, helping to soothe me.

"I do. I also think we need to tell our family."

I move to shake my head, but he runs his fingers through my hair, holding me in place as his arms tighten around me. "Let me finish. We were right not to tell them today. Nothing should overshadow Selena and Keanu's news, but our family deserves to know so they can support us too. That's how we roll, babe, and you need it. You need to be able to talk to Faye and the other girls about it. That is how you will heal."

"I love you," I say against his neck. "I couldn't do life without you."

"Ditto, honeybun." Kal urges my head up, and I clasp his gorgeous face in my hands as his lips descend. We kiss slowly and tenderly for several minutes, and it's almost like I can feel the cracks in my heart gluing themselves back together.

"We'll get through this. We have weathered far harder storms," he says when we finally break apart.

"I know." It's the truth. After what we endured early in our relationship, every other obstacle we have faced has been like a cakewalk. "But this is different. I want more babies with you. I thought I was done, but losing our angel has made me realize I was wrong."

"You know how I have always felt. I love seeing your belly swollen with my child. I would have ten kids if you were up for that."

My eyes pop wide, and I laugh through my dried-up tears. "I draw the line at ten, but I definitely want to try again. The doctor already said it's safe to have sex." They took blood for tests at the hospital the day I underwent a D & C, and we should have the results this week. My ob-gyn said they aren't always able to tell why a woman miscarries. Sometimes it's just one of those things that happens, but after three easy pregnancies, we were not expecting to lose our baby at eleven weeks.

"We could start practicing now." Kal waggles his brows, and I laugh again, my mood infinitely better than it was a few minutes ago.

"I like the way you think, Stinky." I wiggle on his lap, deliberately moving my ass over the semi in his pants. "But we need to have a word about Hewson before we retreat to the bedroom."

Kal exhales heavily, and I thread my fingers through his hair, tilting his head back a little. "Nothing has happened. I just wanted to talk to you about earlier. I really don't think you should be teasing him about girls crawling all over him. That's not exactly helpful and contradictory to the message we have been trying to instill in him about sensible partying and dating."

"That's it though." Kal grips my waist. "There's no such thing as sensible when it comes to parties and women. I'm alienating my son by not being real with him."

I stiffen and pull back a little, putting space between us. "What exactly do you mean, and why is this the first I'm hearing about this?"

"I've been doing a lot of thinking the past few weeks, and I was planning on talking to you, but then you had the miscarriage, and I didn't want to go there."

I climb off his lap and stand. "I'm listening now, so let's hear it." I narrow my eyes at my husband.

Kal rises, reeling me back into his arms, not letting me get away. "We are not fighting about Hewson again, Lana. That's the first thing that has to stop. We are also not talking about this now. It's late, and we're both already emotional."

I collapse against him, knowing he speaks the truth. "I'm sorry, and you're right. This isn't the time. I just worry about him."

"I worry too, but maybe we are overreacting a little and, dare I say it, being too strict because of what we went through."

"It's not like we haven't considered that," I remind him, because we are very much aware of it.

"I know, but I think we need to change our approach. That's really all I'm saying, and you know maybe I wasn't right to say what I said earlier, but sometimes it's so hard to know what the right thing is to say."

"Fact, babe."

A knockout smile spreads across his mouth, momentarily dazzling me. "We're a team, honeybun." Kal nuzzles his nose against mine as he slowly thrusts his hips

34

into my pelvis. "One of the strongest ones I know. We'll figure this out."

I shriek as he scoops me up and throws me over his shoulder. "But right now, all I want to do is make love to my wife and remind her how much I'm still in love with her."

Chapter Four

Kalvin

"**S**pill it," Ky says as we sit across the table from one another in the clubhouse. I quirk a brow as I sip my beer. "I know this morning's shit performance isn't because you have lost your golf swing overnight. I know when you've got something on your mind, so let's hear it."

"It's that obvious?" I trace my finger around the rim of my glass.

"I know you, brother. There hasn't been a single cheesy dad joke told the entire round. That tells me everything."

I flip him the bird. "My dad jokes are legendary. The kids might pretend to hate them, but they secretly love them. You're just jealous."

Kyler holds up a palm. "I only want to help, but if you don't want to talk, that's cool."

I drag my lower lip between my teeth as I stare absently out the window at the gorgeous greens below us. Coming up to my brother's Connecticut cabin for the weekend was a great idea. I already feel less stressed than I have been all week, and I hope it has the same effect on my wife. "Lana is most likely telling Faye this, so I might as well tell you too," I say, swinging my head around and eyeballing my brother. "Lana had a miscarriage three weeks ago, and she's taking it real hard."

Compassion splays across my older brother's face. "I'm so sorry, Kal. I didn't even know you were trying for another."

"We weren't," I truthfully admit. "It was a surprise. I was ecstatic, but Lana wasn't fully on board at first. Now, she's devastated, and I don't know how to help."

"Selena and Keanu's news must have been difficult to hear given the timing." His observation is astute.

"We're really happy for them, but, yeah, it's made it a little tougher for Lana. We were going to tell everyone last week, but we couldn't then."

"How are *you* feeling?" my brother asks, before taking a mouthful of his beer.

"I'm upset too but trying to keep things together for Lana's sake. It doesn't help that we had another full-blown argument with Hewson this week."

"I thought things might have settled down there. He looked happy at dinner."

"He is happy, most of the time. The only time we fight is when he ignores his curfew and comes home late or we catch him sneaking out like we did Wednesday night. Grounding him doesn't work or taking his car keys, which I hate doing 'cause he only just got his driver's license, but he can't keep disrespecting us."

Kyler chuckles, and I momentarily consider

punching him. "Do you ever find it funny we're the ones laying down the law now?"

"All the damn time." I let a grin slip free. "Adulting is hard. Just wait until the twins become teenagers. You think it was hard when they were little and could do nothing for themselves? That's a freaking walk in the park compared to the shit we're dealing with. The thing is, Hewson thinks he's a man. Fuck, he damn well looks like one, and that's half the problem, but we can't just let him do whatever the fuck he wants. He has to have rules."

"Let's get real. We were doing way worse at sixteen. You especially. Your son is practically a saint compared to the shit you were pulling."

"Probably, but that doesn't mean we shouldn't set boundaries and discipline him when he steps outside of them. I love Mom and Dad, and I know they were doing their best, but they let us get away with far too much. I don't want that for my kids. I want them to respect authority and to understand boundaries are there for their protection. Hewson might believe he's a man, but he's not an adult yet, and he still has so much to learn."

"Pity he didn't come this weekend. I could have spoken to him. He might talk to me."

"We had to leave him with Mom and Dad because he was throwing a hissy fit at going out of town for the weekend."

"School starts back in a couple of weeks, so I get he wants to make the most of the end of summer break."

"I think it's more to do with whatever girl is on the scene. Not that he tells me jack shit, but I think he must be dating, and I suspect it's serious. I see him messaging on his phone all the time, and he's always sneaking outside to take calls and coming back with the biggest lovesick expression on his face."

Kyler chuckles. "Man, I wouldn't want to be in his shoes for all the money in the world. I'm glad I have my girl and I'm done with the whole dating scene."

"Fact." I wholeheartedly agree. "I tried talking to him honestly, explaining what a dick I was back in high school and how I didn't see the love of my life when she was right under my nose because I was too busy trying to prove something to myself."

"How did that go down?"

"About as well as you'd expect. I got the whole "that's you, not me" and "don't project your failings onto me. I'm my own person" speech. Part of me was proud. The other part pissed."

Ky drums his fingers on the table. "This whole parenting gig is hard. Cathal has no filter, and he regularly gets into trouble at school for speaking his mind. He got in a physical fight with some other kid at Little League, which really isn't like him, and now Faye is worried there is something driving his behavior."

"What do you think?"

"I spoke to him, and he said there isn't, but I don't know." Tension brackets his face.

"That's a tough one because you don't want to change his personality, but at the same time, he needs to show respect. And if there is something behind it, it's best to get to the root of the problem ASAP."

"Faye wants him to speak to a therapist she's been

recommended. A woman who does a lot of work with kids and teens, but Cathal is refusing to go."

"Sounds like you have your hands full too."

"Tell me about it." Kyler drains his drink. "Life is hectic, but it's good. We're lucky sons of bitches."

"We so are." I drink the last of my beer, throwing a fifty down on the table, before we exit the clubhouse and head toward Kyler's car. "I think I might ask Mom to take the kids for a few days. Lana is going to Paris to attend a book signing her French publisher organized. Maybe I'll go with her, and we can spend a few days in the city of love. It's been years since we took a romantic trip, just the two of us."

"Seriously?" Lana's eyes light up when I mention it to her later that night as we are getting ready for bed.

"No, I'm joking, honeybun," I deadpan before swatting her ass. "Of course, I'm serious. I'm owed a ton of vacation time, and the office is always quieter in August. I don't think I'll have any issue getting a few days off. I'll message Mike in the morning." I pull back the covers on the bed and slide into it.

"You're the best." Lana flings herself at me, straddling my thighs as she wraps her arms around my neck and dots kisses all over my face. "And you definitely deserve a reward." She pins me with a suggestive look as a broad smile graces her delectable mouth.

"You seem happier since we arrived," I admit,

parking the reward comment for a few minutes. I gently cup her cheek. "Did you speak to Faye?"

She nods. "I did. We talked about it at length, and I instantly felt better." I try not to feel insulted Faye's words soothed my wife when mine didn't because the most important thing is she seems happier. "Kal." She tips my chin up. "Faye reinforced everything you have been saying, and it's not that I didn't listen when you said it. It's that I needed time to process it. Hearing what the doctor said this week helped too. To know it wasn't anything I did or didn't do. That there is no conclusive medical reason for what happened. It's just one of those things. What's most important is that we have three beautiful, healthy children and no reason why we can't have more."

"I love you so much." I press a kiss to the underside of her jaw.

"I love you too, babe." Leaning down, she places a soft, loving kiss on my lips. "I will always remember the baby we lost, but I'm not consumed with grief anymore. Even this shit with Hewson will blow over. He's got a good head on his shoulders, and maybe we need to let him make some mistakes even if the lessons he learns are hard on him."

"I have come to the same conclusion. He still has rules he must abide by, but I was thinking about it. What if we sat down with him and asked what he felt was reasonable for us, as parents, to implement, and maybe we could meet him halfway?"

"A compromise," my wife says, her smile expanding. "I like that, and I think our son will too. At least, he will see we are trying to understand and to find some middle ground."

"Now that's all sorted, let's discuss my reward," I say, sliding my hands underneath the hem of her silk nightgown and palming her ass.

"What did you have in mind?" She waggles her brows while grinding on top of me.

"This bed, no clothes, lots of dirty talk, and filthy, sweaty sex."

"I'm speaking your language," Lana purrs, pulling her nightgown up and tossing it away.

"Hell yeah, baby." Grabbing her hips, I flip her on to her back on the bed before kicking my sleep pants away and crawling back over her gorgeous naked body. Pushing her thighs apart, I kneel before the gates of heaven and lick my lips. "Prepare to be fucked like you've never been fucked before."

Chapter Five

Faye

I poke my head into Cathal's room, not in the least bit surprised to find him slouched in his gaming chair in front of the TV, playing *The Last Guardian* on his PlayStation. His siblings are all out for the count, exhausted after the journey from Boston to Dublin. But Cathal has boundless energy, and he seems to require little sleep. "Don't stay up too late," I say, tiptoeing across the varnished hardwood floor toward my son. "Remember we're spending the day at Brad and Rachel's house tomorrow."

"I hadn't forgotten," he says, not lifting his gaze from the screen as his fingers move like lightning on the game controller. I must be the most uncoordinated person on the planet because I cannot get my fingers to work quick enough anytime I play a game with my son. Cathal is a pro, and he seemed to master the basics superfast. He regularly beats Ky at those football and basketball games they play. Ky is equal parts proud and frustrated. Those

Kennedy competitive genes are still alive and thriving in my husband's DNA, that's for sure.

Wrapping my arms around my son from behind, I lean in and press a kiss to his cheek. "Night, honey."

"Night, Mom."

"Love you."

He briefly lifts his head, his big blue eyes smiling as he looks at me. "Love you too." He returns his focus to the game as I plant a kiss on top of his dark head. "And stop worrying. I'm fine," he adds.

"Moms never stop worrying. It's part of our job."

He rolls his eyes, and I smile to myself as I exit his bedroom, padding quietly along the hallway and down the stairs. My smile expands as I pass the myriad of framed family photos adorning the walls. Ky teases me relentlessly because I'm always taking pictures of the kids, and we literally have thousands stored in the cloud. I want to capture every precious moment because they are growing up so fast, and I don't want to forget a single second. In part, my obsession could be the consequence of losing my parents when I was young and hating how few captured memories there are of the first seventeen years of my life. Mom preferred to live in the moment rather than render a permanent image. I respect her for that, but it's hard now they are gone and my memories aren't always reliable. I think my need to document everything stems from that hole existing inside me.

"There you are," my husband says, walking down the hallway toward me. "I was just coming to find you." Kyler winds his arms around my waist and rests his chin on top of my head. "Is everything okay?"

I place my hands on his strong, muscular arms, savoring the warmth and solidity of his touch. "Everything is fine. I just got nostalgic looking at our pictures."

"Do you regret selling your parents' house?" he asks, turning me around in his arms.

I slide my arms up his chest and around his neck as his hands encircle my back. "It still makes me sad, but it was the right decision. Our family had outgrown it, and this house fits our needs much better." I sold the house I grew up in when I was pregnant with Connor, our youngest. Every summer, we take a vacation in Ireland because it's important to me that my kids acknowledge the Irish part of their heritage. We visit my parents' graves, visit my grandparents in Wexford, hang out with my dad, Adam, if he makes the trip, organize a beach day at Brittas Bay, visit some of the tourist spots, and take in a couple of shows. The kids love it. Even more so the past two summers because we get to hang out with Brad and Rachel and their kids.

My bestie relocated eighteen months ago because Brad needed to be based in Ireland or the UK for business. I miss Rach something fierce, so these summer holidays are crucial. We usually spend three or four weeks here, but we stayed in Massachusetts later than usual because we wanted to be there to see Selena receive her award, and then we spent a week at our Connecticut cabin, so we are only here for ten days this time.

"You seem troubled." His fingers tuck pieces of my hair behind my ears. "Is it Cathal's diagnosis?"

I exhale deeply as I rest my head on my husband's chest and hold him close. "Partly, but it's more than that.

"Let's sit outside and talk. I already have a bottle of wine on ice." He runs his hand up and down my back in a soothing gesture before taking my hand and leading me outside.

After we bought this new build in County Wicklow, we hired landscape gardeners to completely redesign the large back garden. Now, we have a decked area with a large table and an abundance of comfortable seating. Colorful flowerbeds and shrubs run along the entire perimeter of the garden and are dotted throughout the lush grass. A massive playground occupies prime real estate in the middle of the space with swings, a slide, a climbing frame, and a trampoline.

One of my favorite things to do is to sit out under the stars and enjoy the peace and quiet of our surroundings. August in Ireland is warm, but it's not warm enough to sit outside late at night without heating, so I'm glad to see my thoughtful husband has already lit the patio heaters.

I get comfortable on the couch while Ky pours two glasses of white wine and hands one to me. I snuggle into his side as I sip my drink, enjoying the companionable silence before I voice the decision I have made.

"I love you," he says, circling his arm tighter around my shoulders. "I think I know what you need to say, and you shouldn't be afraid to say it." He tilts my chin up with one finger. "I've got your back, babe. Always. Whatever you need, you've got it."

Tears pool in my eyes. Sometimes, I wonder how the hell I got so lucky to have this man in my life. "You're still my everything, Ky. I hope you know that," I say through blurry vision, emotion getting the better of me.

"I do, and it's the same for me. Life may be hectic, and we may not get as much time together as we'd like, but I never doubt your love. I feel it every day, Faye." He sweeps wispy strands of my long dark hair off my face. "I see it every time I look at our beautiful, amazing children."

My heart swells with love, like it does anytime I think about our kids. "We did good, didn't we?"

"We did." He kisses me and it's infinitely tender.

When we break our lip-lock, I tell him what's on my mind. "I want to give up my job."

"I know."

I arch a brow. "You do?"

He nods before taking a drink of his wine. "I think you wanted to give it up two years ago when Mom sold the company, but you felt you'd be letting the staff down if you didn't stay, at least while they were transitioning to new management."

Setting my wineglass down, I press a fierce kiss to his gorgeous lips and fling my arms around his neck. "I love how well you know me. I even love that you knew it back then but didn't say anything because you didn't want to interfere. I love how you let me make my own choices and how eagerly you support me. I know a lot of husbands are not like that." Jill's estranged husband pops into my mind, but I force that asshole's image out, not wanting to think about him when I'm sharing a moment with my man. "I feel so lucky to have you, Ky." Tears stab my eyes again, and if Ky hadn't had the snip last year, I'd honestly wonder if I was pregnant because I've been super hormonal lately. I think it might just be stress, and there isn't anything good about that.

"Ditto, babe." He kisses the tip of my nose. "What is your plan?"

I worry my lower lip between my teeth. "I want to stay home with the kids. They are growing up too quickly, and a lot of time, I feel like I'm squeezing them in around work, and that doesn't sit right with me."

"You shouldn't feel guilty. The kids don't feel like that. They are healthy and happy, for the most part. They aren't neglected, and you see how they adore you. You're a great mom, Faye. Please don't ever doubt that."

"God, would you stop?" I playfully swat at his chest as more tears well in my eyes. "I'm going to be bawling in five seconds."

He puts his wineglass down and hauls me into his lap. "I know these are happy tears, but don't cry, honey." He swipes his thumbs under my eyes, brushing the dampness away. "I think it's amazing you want to do this and I'm all for it, as long as it's what'll make you happy."

"It is." I chew on the inside of my mouth.

"Out with it."

"Do you think it's stupid to throw away my education and just give up a career I enjoy? Because I do enjoy working in human resource management. I love helping people to develop their potential, and it's so rewarding watching people succeed and kicking ass. But I'm not enjoying working for the company any longer. I hate what they have done to the culture. How they have driven out many good people, and I fucking hate working for that asshole Mark. He'll probably throw a party the day I resign because I know this is what he was hoping for."

Ky peers deep into my eyes. "I suspect you haven't told me the half of what's gone down."

"I haven't because I knew how you'd react, and punching the new CEO would only get you arrested. Trust me, that dickhead is not worth getting a rap sheet over."

"I hate that jerk, and punching him would be highly enjoyable, but there are smarter ways to retaliate." His eyes twinkle with dark delight.

"Tempting as that is, do *not* call Keven. I'm pretty sure karma will bite Mark in the ass one of these days, and when it happens, I'll be cheering from the sidelines."

"I wouldn't be too hasty. It seems like Kev's FBI days arc drawing to a close, and the line of work he's going into would perfectly align to our goals. He'd be more than happy to take that jerk down."

"I know he would, but promise me you'll drop it, and you can't mention anything to your mom either. It would kill her and Brad's mom to know what has become of the company they nurtured to success."

He sighs. "She probably already knows. While it would upset her, Mom is happily retired. I don't think it would upset her for too long. She'll be more upset that you have stayed out of some misguided loyalty to her, and she'd be furious to hear how Mark has been treating you."

"She doesn't need to know. I'm going to call him in the morning and quit. I'll email my resignation later after I get off the phone." A layer of stress lifts from my shoulders. "It's amazing how much lighter I already feel."

"Good. I've been worried about you. And to answer your previous question, it's not wrong of you to pause your career to spend time with our children. You're not wasting your education or your experience. You can always go back to work when the kids are older, if you like, or you could set up your own consultancy business. If this is what you need to do, don't waste another second feeling guilty. Things happen for a reason."

"I love you, Mr. Kennedy." I straddle his thighs and grind my pussy against his cock. "And I'm going to spend the rest of the night showing you just how much."

Chapter Six
Kyler

Blinking my tired eyes open, I prop my body up on my elbows, a moan slipping from my lips as the vision of my gorgeous sexy wife comes into view. "Morning, babe," Faye says from her position in between my legs. Her slender fingers are wrapped around my morning wood as she jerks me off, exactly how I like it.

"Fuck," I hiss, my cock jumping eagerly as I watch the love of my life lower her lips over my erection. Faye's warm mouth lavishes attention on my dick, and I fall back against the bed, contemplating what a lucky fucking bastard I am to have such a goddess for my wife. My hips rise off the bed as she takes me deep into her mouth, my cock hitting the back of her throat. My fingers dive in her hair as I hold her face to my groin.

Her fingers are curled around the base of my shaft as she expertly sucks my dick. My wife gives the best fucking head, and I crave her touch as much as I did at the start. Sex has only gotten better over the years, but we don't get to indulge as much as we'd like. Two busy jobs and four kids under eleven tends to wreak havoc with our sex life. Perhaps that will change now Faye has chosen to give up work for a while.

A familiar tingling hits my lower spine, and I wrap Faye's hair around my fist and tug gently. "Ride me, baby. I want to come inside you." The best thing about the vasectomy is sex without condoms. Faye was having issues taking the pill, so she stopped, and I fucking hated using condoms. I want to feel my wife's walls hugging my dick when I fuck her, and now I get to experience that all the time.

Faye climbs on top of me, and we both groan as she situates herself on my dick. "Stop," I command when she starts moving up and down. "You know the rules, beautiful." I tug at the hem of her silk nightdress. "I want you naked. Take this off."

Since she gave birth to Connor, she's been a little body conscious, which I hate. My wife is stunning—even more gorgeous than the day I married her. The extra flesh and stretch marks on her stomach remind me of the precious gifts she carried in her womb, and nothing gets me harder than the evidence of my kids on my wife's body. I don't understand why she doesn't realize how utterly beautiful she is, and I try to remind her any chance I get.

"That's better," I say, my greedy eyes drinking her in as she moves on top of me, fully naked. My fingers dance up her stomach, along her rib cage, and over her tits. I squeeze the supple skin while dragging my thumbs back and forth across her hard nipples until she's writhing and moaning on top of me. I thrust up inside her as she rocks up and down on my dick, our movements in perfect synchronization, and I just admire the exquisite view.

"You look so hot fucking my dick," I tell her, licking my lips as I fondle her tits and gaze in awe at the gorgeous sight.

"God, Ky. This feels so good."

She told me that last night, over and over, as we spent hours making love, into the early hours, before falling into a deep sleep. Waking to her hands on my body is my favorite way to wake up, and as long as I live, I will never get enough of her touch.

Faye's long dark hair is knotted from my hands, hanging sexily down her back and over one shoulder. Her tempting curves mold to my hands as I explore every inch of her silky skin before bringing my fingers to her clit. I massage the sensitive bundle of nerves as I thrust up harder inside her.

But I need more.

Gripping her hips, I flip us over until I'm on top and she's spread-eagled underneath me. Leaning down, I kiss her passionately as her legs curl around my waist. I drive into her in long, slow, deep thrusts, savoring the way she feels wrapped around my cock. "You're so beautiful. So sexy, and I'm so in love with you," I tell her when we surface for air.

"I have the sexiest, sweetest, most romantic husband in the world, and I'm the luckiest bitch."

Words are redundant after that as I fuck her into the bed before taking us both over the ledge. We have only just finished, collapsed in a tangle of limbs on the bed, when the door creeps open. Faye shrieks, yanking the covers up over us in the nick of time.

"Mommy. Ciara says I can't have pancakes." Connor pouts as he races across the room and throws himself on top of us on the bed.

"I told him we are having breakfast at Elodie's house," Ciara says, storming into the room. "But he won't believe me."

Connor lies down on Faye over the covers, pinning her with big blue doe eyes. "But I'm hungry. The tummy monster will get me if I don't feed it."

I chuckle, messing up his dark hair. "We can't have that. Tell you what, you can have one pancake each before we leave."

His cute little face lights up. "Yay!" He pokes his tongue out at his sister. "Told ya!"

Ciara rolls her eyes. "You are such a softie, Dad."

"That's not a bad thing," Faye says, dotting kisses into Connor's head before he scrambles off the bed. "Watch your brother while Daddy and I get dressed," she tells our eleven-year-old. "And wake your twin and Caoimhe if they aren't up already. We need to leave soon."

An hour later and we're packed up for the drive to Clontarf, where Brad and Rachel have a gorgeous split-level bungalow.

We manage to miss most of the rush-hour traffic and make it in less than an hour. I punch the code into the gates and slowly drive down the short driveway, the sun glistening high in the sky as our friends' home comes into view.

I pull up in front of the house and kill the engine.

"Remember," Faye says, turning around and eyeing Cathal in the back. "Be nice to Elodie."

He makes a circular motion on the top of his head. "I'll be a saint. I promise."

I seriously doubt he has it in him, but I know he'll try. Poor Elodie has the biggest crush on our son, but he's more interested in the inner mechanics of motorbikes than girls, but I'm sure that will change soon.

Rachel rushes out of the house, and Faye leaps from the car, the two women racing toward one another with obvious excitement.

Brad and Rach flew home for the awards ceremony, but we barely got to see them before they had to fly back. I know Faye misses having her friend close by, and it always warms my heart to see them together. They embrace in a huge hug as I climb out from behind the wheel and stretch my arms over my head.

"Someone's getting a little flabby," Brad says, lightly punching my stomach.

"As if." I scoff, narrowing my eyes at my best friend while lifting the hem of my T-shirt. I palm my toned abs. "Abs of steel, dude."

"Good to see you, man." Brad pulls me into a hug, and we slap each other on the back.

"You too. Wish it wasn't such a short visit this time." We only have ten days in Ireland because we need to get home to get the kids ready for school.

"We'll make the best of it." Brad greets the kids, ushering everyone inside while I inspect my friend. Bruising shadows linger in the space under his eyes, and he's got at least a few days' worth of stubble on his chin and cheeks. His eyes look tired, and he carries defeat in the way his shoulders slump. I suspected something is up the last time we talked on the phone, but I see it on his face now as clear as day, and I vow to get it out of him before it's time for us to leave.

Rachel has a gorgeous brunch laid out in the garden, and conversation is casual as we catch up over the delicious feast. After, the kids play on the swings and slide before changing into their swimwear.

Elodie is a strong swimmer and a rising star on the local swim team, so Rach and Brad had a covered pool built on the grounds. Kal designed it for them, so it is well suited for their needs. A covered tunnel runs from the house to the pool house so they don't have to go outside to access it in the rainy winter. During the summer, the side windows on the righthand side fully retract, bringing the outside in.

The girls watch over the kids while Brad and I clean up the kitchen, and then we grab a couple of beers and move outside to relieve our wives. They head out for a walk at a nearby park while we sink onto seats on the patio just outside the pool area. The kids are having the time of their lives playing water volleyball, laughing and screaming as each team tries to out skill the other. Brad slides sunglasses on as he says, "Rachel was telling me you took Cathal to see a psychologist. Is everything okay?"

I kick my feet up on the low coffee table, stretching out my legs as I reply. "We were a little concerned with some of his behavior, so we wanted him to talk to someone, to see if there were any issues we needed to be aware of."

Brad sits up straighter, angling his head in my direction. "You think something's going on?"

I know where his head has wandered because it's where my head wandered to at first. "I did, initially. But I wasn't sure if I was reading too much into it, you know?"

He nods. "It makes sense you'd be hyper vigilant after what happened to you as a kid."

"I am. The thought of anyone harming my kids sends me into a murderous rage." I gulp back a mouthful of beer to smother the dark thoughts threatening to bubble to the surface.

"Me too. We had an issue with one of the girls at Elodie's school. She was bullying her, and I wanted to throttle the little brat when I found out. Lo didn't say anything for weeks, until Rach finally got her to open up. We went straight to the school and got it sorted."

"I'm sorry to hear that. How is Lo now?"

Brad emits a low chuckle. "Still smitten, if the lovesick look on her face right now is any indication."

I glance over at the pool, chuckling as I watch Elodie beam at Cathal. Though our eldest kids are all the same age, our twins are a good head taller than Brad and Rachel's only daughter. "Wouldn't it be funny if we ended up in-laws at some point in the future?"

A shudder works its way through Brad. "Jeez, man. Don't even go there. I can't think about my princess dating without wanting to go outside and punch something."

"Tell me about it. I have double the heartache lying

in wait, and I already know Caoimhe is going to test my patience to the limit," I say, watching our six-year-old flirt and giggle with Roan, Brad's five-year-old son.

"Fun times ahead." Brad raises his bottle in a salute.

"For sure."

"So, what's up with Cathal?"

"He's intellectually gifted, or so the psychologist says. It's why he's been increasingly frustrated at school. He's way ahead of all his classmates and finding it hard to relate to them. The coursework is not stimulating enough, and he's full of this restless energy that has nowhere to go." I wouldn't ordinarily say this to people, because I'm sure it would come off as bragging, but Brad is family, and I can tell him anything. "He can explain the inner workings of a motorcycle, in minute detail, if you ask. He knows the name of every solar system, and he can give you an explicit biography of every character in the Artemis Fowl series in alphabetical order. He absorbs information. Soaks it up like a sponge."

"I'm not surprised to hear that. I remember how amazing his vocabulary was at two, and at three, you could hold an intelligent conversation with him. He always has his nose in a book, and it's clear he observes the world around him and retains the information. It makes sense when you think about it."

A pregnant pause descends, shattered in seconds by shrieks and giggles from the pool. "I can't imagine what it must be like to have a brain that is constantly spinning and craving knowledge," I say. "It's no wonder he's been lashing out and frustrated."

"What can you do?"

"We have to adapt how we treat him, in subtle ways. We want to encourage and support his development while still ensuring he has boundaries. We're talking to the school about moving him up a grade or two, and I'm trying to convince Faye to let him join our local motocross team, but she's worried about the risks."

"It's not an easy sport to embrace, but you were a natural, and he's clearly interested."

"That doesn't necessarily mean he'll be any good. He hasn't shown a prowess for any sport so far. He freaking sucks at Little League, but I can't fault his determination to better himself. Maybe he won't enjoy motocross, but he deserves the opportunity to at least try."

"Faye will come around. She lives for those kids."

"She does, and I know she will. I'm going to take her to the track one Saturday so she can see what's involved. I know the guy who owns the place—I used to race against him—and he manages the junior team. I'm hoping to grab him for a quick talk. I think he'll help to set Faye's mind at ease."

"How are things with you two?" Removing his glasses, he rubs the bridge of his nose.

"Great. Couldn't be better. Faye has decided to give up work and spend time at home with the kids. I think that's going to make a huge difference in our lives."

"That's awesome, man. Maybe you can cut back on some of that crazy overtime you've been doing."

"That's not the norm. We have been busier than usual, thanks to the enhanced visibility from the award. But I hired a couple of extra people, and I have a solid team. I spoke to Sel last week about doing more remote working from home, and she was all for it. It means we can escape to the cabin or the beach house for long week-ends or during school breaks."

Brad sighs. "I'm envious. That sounds amazing."

"What aren't you saying?" I ask, eyeballing him.

He swallows hard, taking a long swig of his beer, before facing me with troubled eyes. "I'm worried about my marriage. Honestly, if something doesn't change, I'm not sure we're gonna make it."

Chapter Seven
Brad

Anguish is a heavy layer coating the back of my throat as I put a voice to my fears. Kyler won't judge, and I need to confide in someone. But we can't have this conversation in earshot of the kids when the women could return at any second. So, I ask my buddy to park it until later.

"I was thinking we could ask the guys to sleep over," I tell my wife as I'm removing meat from the refrigerator later. "I know you want to have your girl time with Faye, and Ky and I were thinking of heading out for a few beers."

"That sounds like a plan," Rachel says, sidestepping me as she reaches for the salad ingredients.

"I'll mention it to Ky outside."

"Okay." Rach closes the fridge with one hip, waves of glossy dark hair tumbling around her face. After years of wearing her hair red, she returned to her natural dark-brown roots at the start of the summer. The day before we were due to fly to Ireland for the awards ceremony, she returned home having chopped her long locks in half. Now, her hair sits just below her chin, and she has never looked more gorgeous or seemed more out of my reach.

"What?" she asks, and I realize I've just been standing here staring at her.

"You look beautiful." I cup one side of her face. "I love your hair like this, and your dress is pretty."

"It's from my new summer line," she supplies. "You know I love to test every item myself. This is one of my favorites. I love the simplicity of the design and how comfortable it is."

It's a basic white summer dress with thin straps and a scalloped lace hem, but I can tell the material is high quality and the cut is exquisite. It helps that my gorgeous wife has a body to die for. She could wear a sack and make it look good. On the average woman, this dress would probably look plain. Rachel elevates it to something special. "I'm betting it's a best seller."

"It is." Pride underscores her words, as it should. Rachel has worked hard to build her business from the ground up, and she deserves every inch of her success. Her eyes light up whenever she talks about her business, and it's the only time she is animated with me these days.

"I love you," I blurt, hating that I can't remember the last time I said it. Without stopping to second-guess myself, I reel her into my arms, half afraid she'll reject me and thrilled when she doesn't. Rachel wraps herself around me, almost clinging to me in a way that feels desperate. Which confuses me, because that's not my wife.

"I love you too," she whispers, her voice sounding

hoarse. "I don't want to lose you," she adds, and every muscle in my body locks up tight.

"You can't lose me. That's an impossibility. I'm yours. Always," I truthfully reply, holding her closer and burying my nose in her hair. Delicate strawberry and peach smells tickle my nostrils, the familiarity helping to soothe the frayed edges of my nerves.

"Is that—"

"Auntie Rachel!" Ciara exclaims, barging into the kitchen and cutting across whatever my wife was about to say. "We need more lemonade." Ciara holds the empty plastic jug aloft, waving it in our direction.

Rachel eases out of my arms and walks away. The moment is lost. I stifle my frustration as I grab the meat cartons and wander outside to the grill.

A couple of hours later, I finally get a chance to unload to my best friend and ask for his advice as we sit in an alcove in my local bar, nursing two pints of creamy Guinness.

"Tell me what's going on with you and Rach. You shocked the shit out of me earlier," Ky says, worry etched upon his face.

"We have been drifting apart for a while. It doesn't help we're like passing ships in the night. I get home from a business trip, and then it's her turn to travel for work. In between trips, we are juggling crazy busy jobs and the kids, and we are both so stressed and overworked that we barely have any time to spend together. At night, we fall into bed, both of us asleep before our heads have hit the pillow. I can't remember the last time we had sex, and I'm ashamed to say when I told her I loved her earlier it was the first time in a long time." I pause my verbal diarrhea to draw a breath, burying my head in my hands, as emotion threatens to overwhelm me.

Ky squeezes my shoulder in a show of support, but he doesn't say anything, understanding there is more I need to get out.

I look up at him through blurry eyes, and I'm too tired to care how much of a pussy I must look. "I'm scared I've lost her. Outside of those issues, it seems like she isn't interested in me anymore. Our conversations revolve around who will pick up the kids and drive them wherever they need to be. On weekends, when we manage to grab a couple of hours in front of the TV, conversation is either nonexistent or we talk about work or mundane stuff. Anything but the things we need to talk about."

My chest heaves as pain spreads across it. "I held her today, and for the first time in ages, she welcomed it. It took everything I had not to burst into tears because hugging my wife felt so damn good, and I realize how starved I am for her touch." Tears prick my eyes and I look away, ashamed to be falling apart in front of my friend even if he has seen me during some of my darkest days. "I'm failing, man. I'm failing at my most important role. I'm a shitty husband who can't even talk to his wife, and it's killing me."

Ky grabs me into a hug, and I use the time to get a grip on myself. We pull back, and I scrub at my eyes before lifting my Guinness to my lips and drinking greedily.

"I had no idea things were like that though the strain was obvious today. It's shit man, but all isn't lost. You still love each other, and that's the main thing. It would be a whole other ball game if the love was gone."

"I don't know if she loves me anymore, Ky," I admit in a defeated tone.

"She loves you." His confident tone rings out loud and clear. "After you said what you did at lunchtime, I observed her on the down low the rest of the day. She's hurting, man. I see it in her eyes. Rach has always been good at putting on a front and hiding her pain, which is why I haven't seen it before, but when you really look, you can see it. You don't hurt like that if there's no love."

I shrug because, honestly, I don't know anything anymore.

"It's more than that though. I saw the way she was looking at you. She loves you. It's clear as day. I don't know where you two went wrong, but not loving one another isn't the problem."

"How do I fix this? I feel so lost."

"I don't know, but you've got to start by talking to her. Properly talking to her. You need to tell her how you are feeling. She needs to know you love her and you want to fix things. And you need to find out what she's feeling and if there is anything behind this."

"I need a plan of action."

"You do." His brow puckers as he considers it. "How about this? We'll take the kids back with us tomorrow. We'll keep them overnight. Spend the day talking with Rachel. Thrash it all out and then worship her all night. Remind her of what you guys have. Reconnect on every level and hopefully you'll know where to go from there."

Hope blooms inside me, and I'm regretting not

confiding in my buddy sooner. Ky isn't saying anything I didn't know deep down myself, but I needed someone to voice it. "Rach has to go into the office for a meeting in the morning, so maybe I'll surprise her and take her out to lunch. Then we can head back to the house to talk." My mind churns with ideas. "I'll get her some flowers and those Leonidas chocolates she loves, and I'll get her a voucher for the spa at the nearby hotel. She hasn't been for a treatment in ages."

"She'll appreciate all those gestures, I'm sure."

"That's only surface level though. If we're to repair the damage to our marriage, I think we need to make some big changes." I take another drink before I articulate this next truth. "I think I'm going to quit my job."

Ky's eyes pop wide.

"We don't have to talk about it, if it puts you in an awkward position," I blurt, not having thought it through. I am the European sales director of the golf company Ky's brother Kaden jointly owns with his wife, Eva. I have worked for them for years, and they've been good to me, but lately I have been feeling more and more unsettled.

"You're my best friend. What you tell me I will keep confidential. You need to get this shit off your chest, man. Give it to me."

"I haven't enjoyed my job the past eighteen months. I miss the US. I miss you guys and the rest of my family. I'm sick of all the traveling, and I know it's getting to Rachel too. She has a management team in place in New York, but she really needs to be there. She has never complained or blamed me. She readily agreed to move here when Kade and Eva asked me to relocate. It's not that we're unhappy in Ireland, but it's not home. For me or for Rachel."

"Talk to Kade and Eva. Tell them this. I bet they'll replace you here and find another role for you back home. They won't want to lose you."

"Your brother and his wife have been really good to me, Ky, and I don't want to let them down, but I feel the time has come to try something new."

"You've got to do what's best for you and your family. As long as you give them notice and explain it as you've explained it to me, I am sure there will be no bad feelings between you. They wouldn't want to come between you and Rachel, upset your family, or have you working a role you don't enjoy anymore."

"I hope you're right because the last thing I want to do is fall out with them when they have given me so much."

I rub my sweaty palms down the side of my jeans as I stand in the elevator, watching the floors disappear as we ascend higher, clutching a massive bouquet of colorful flowers in my hands while it feels like my heart might tear from my chest at any minute it's pounding that fast. The plan I hatched last night with Kyler is in full swing, but an attack of last-minute nerves has me second-guessing myself. Rachel is always crazy busy; what if she doesn't appreciate the gesture? What if she gets annoyed at me interfering in her work and showing up like this?

The elevator pings, and the doors slowly open, and I guess the time for backing out is gone. Thrusting my shoulders forward, I regain my confidence as I step out into the plush lobby. My heart bursts with pride at the sight of the huge Rachel McConaughey logo on the back wall behind the reception desk, and I am in awe of my wife's brilliance.

"Mr. McConaughey." Eleana's eyes pop wide as I loom over her, her fingers flying over the keyboard. "Did you have an appointment? I don't see you on the schedule." She looks all flustered, and I feel for the young woman. The last time I was here, she had only just started the job. I thought her nerves were because she was new, but I think she must have a nervous disposition.

Majella stands from her seat on the other side of the newer, younger receptionist. "Brad doesn't need an appointment to see his wife, Eleana." Her smile is kind as she gently chastises the girl.

Eleana's cheeks flare bright red. "Of course, I'm sorry, sir."

"It's Brad, and no apologies are necessary. Is Rachel free now or still in her meeting?"

"The meeting ended fifteen minutes ago. You can go in to her," Majella says, staring dreamily at the bouquet in my hands. "Rachel is a lucky woman."

I'm not sure she'd agree with that sentiment anymore, but I nod and smile respectfully at Rachel's office manager. I know Rachel thinks the world of Majella, and she goes above and beyond to keep my wife sane. Really, I should have brought flowers for her too.

I punch the code into the wall-mounted keypad, and

the frosted glass double doors open, admitting me to the main floor. The large room is divided in three. To the left are the rooms where the interior design team works. In the middle is where the office-based staff resides, and the right-hand side of the space is where the meeting rooms and private offices are situated.

A few heads lift, and piercing stares almost burn a hole in the back of my shirt as I walk across the room. A few people I know say hello, and I return their greetings, noticing how transparent the visible urgency is in the room. A hum of excitement purrs in the air, and I can tell it's a vibrant working environment and the staff truly enjoys their jobs. I have missed that, and I know if I was to be completely honest with myself I stopped loving my job long before I accepted the role and transfer to Ireland. Pity I hadn't given it more consideration at the time, but my need to provide for my family has underpinned a lot of my decisions, not all of them smart.

Seeing what my mom went through with my dad left an indelible black mark on my soul. I swore a long time ago to sacrifice everything to ensure I could provide for my family.

Yet, the last thing I ever intended to sacrifice is my wife's happiness or my marriage, and I think I have a lot of introspection to do.

But, like Ky said, it's not too late. As long as we still love each other and are committed to our marriage, we can overcome the other obstacles.

Rach's office is the first one in this area, and I make a beeline for it, knocking firmly on the wooden door. I don't want to barge in, in case anyone is inside with my wife.

The blinds are drawn on the glass windows, shielding the office from view. I frown when there is no response to my knock, wondering if Rachel is actually in there. Not wanting to look like a prize prick, standing stupidly outside his wife's office holding a bunch of flowers, I turn the handle and walk into the room, slamming to a halt when I see my wife bent over her desk, sobbing her heart out.

I quickly close the door and stride toward her. "Rachel! What's wrong?" She doesn't look up, continuing to cry, her shoulders heaving as her body wracks with huge sobs. I don't know if she has even heard me. I place the flowers down and round her desk, crouching in front of her. I reach for her arm. "Sweetheart. It's me. Please tell me what's wrong?"

Rachel stills, and her sobs stop as she slowly lifts her chin. Angling her head, she stares at me through swollen red-rimmed eyes. "Brad?" she croaks, looking from me to the flowers and back again. "What are you doing here?" She sniffles, straightening up, and I unfurl to my full height, leaning my butt against the desk as I watch my clearly distressed wife with a stabbing pain in my heart.

If I have caused this, I don't know if I can forgive myself.

"I came to surprise you. I wanted to take you out for lunch and ... never mind that now. Why are you crying? Is this because of me, or has someone done something to hurt you?" I swear if any asshole has upset her, I will lay them out flat.

"We won the Tribeca contract," she says.

"Congratulations. I know how badly you wanted it."

"I did. I do." She corrects herself, removing a tissue packet from her top drawer. "It's a great thing."

"So, why the tears?"

With soft, deliberate movements, I brush damp strands of hair back off her face.

"I don't know if I can do this anymore," she wails. Her lower lip wobbles, and more tears pool in her eyes.

I drop to my knees, swiveling her chair around so we're facing one another. I take her hands in one hand and cup her face with the other as I stare into pained eyes. "Talk to me. Tell me what's going on."

"It's all so overwhelming, and I'm so goddamn tired all the time. I'm sick of traveling and working such long hours and fitting the kids around our hectic schedules. I love being my own boss and how much my brand is growing, but I didn't think it would be at the extent of everything else in my life. What good is success if we have to sacrifice so much? We barely see one another, and when we do, it's—" She breaks down in tears, and her sobs tear strips off my heart.

I wrap my arms around her, holding her tight, fighting the urge to cry too. My wife needs me now. This isn't about me. It's about soothing Rach, and I would move mountains to remove her pain. It's tangible and I can't believe I have let this go on so long. That I have buried my head in the sand and refused to confront what was directly in front of my eyes. I have so much to make up to her. I have been a shitty husband, but I'm determined to fix things. I love her so much, and I can't bear the thought of losing her. She is my entire world. Rachel, Elodie, and Roan are who I live for, and I will fight tooth and nail to hold on to my family.

"It's awful," she finishes, peering into my eyes. "I feel like there's this big void between us and we're so far apart. I could cope with the work stress if it didn't feel like I was losing you." Conviction flares in her eyes as her tears dry up. She looks directly into my eyes when she says, "I know, Brad. I know you're having an affair."

Chapter Eight
Rachel

S hock splays across Brad's face as he stares at me. "Baby, I'm not cheating on you. Why the hell would you think that?" Confusion gives way to horrified realization as I watch emotions play across his gorgeous face. "Is this about *Jenna*?"

I nod as more tears well in my eyes. Fuck, I'm such a basket case. Lately, it doesn't take much to instigate tears. I don't know if it's lack of sleep, work-related stress, or the constant fear I've been living with these past few months since I discovered my husband kissing his assistant. Now he's saying he's not having an affair? His reaction seems genuine, but do I truly know him anymore?" "I saw you two together. I called over to your office one night. You'd been working late all week. It was the time you had all those issues with the new website. Jill came over to mind the kids so I could surprise you. I grabbed some food from our favorite Italian restaurant, and I planned to keep you company while you worked, only I was the one who ended up surprised."

"I don't know what you saw, but it's not what you think."

"You were kissing her, Brad!" Anger flares inside, surging to the surface after months of tamping it all down inside. "Her arms were around your neck, and she was pressed all up against you. I almost threw up on the spot."

"Rachel, my God." Tears well in his eyes. "Why didn't you say anything?"

"Have you any idea what seeing that did to me?! Have you?" I shout, losing control of my tenuous emotions.

"Baby. I wasn't kissing her. She threw herself at me. Caught me completely off guard. You must have arrived at that exact moment, and I'm guessing you left straight-away because if you'd stayed you would have seen me push her away and tell her to leave."

I snort out a laugh. "Of course, you'd say that. Don't all married men lie when confronted with the truth of their affair?"

"Rachel, I swear to you on our kids' lives I am not having an affair. I'm telling the truth. We have cameras in the office. I'll pull up the footage, and you can watch it if you don't believe me."

"What about all the overtime you've been doing? You are rarely home before nine at night. I know you used to work late during busy periods but never consistently like lately."

"Oh my God, honey." He rests his forehead against mine. "You think I was with her?"

Tears spill down my cheeks as I nod.

"No, baby. I called Kade the instant she left the

building and explained what had happened. It wasn't the first time she hit on me though it was the first time she kissed me. I repeatedly rejected her. Told her I loved my wife and I wasn't interested. Warned her if she didn't stop she'd be out of a job. I fired her immediately, and the reason I've been working overtime is because I'm doing her job and mine. I haven't been able to find someone to replace her, and though I have temp agency assistants from time to time, the bulk of that work now rests on my shoulders."

"Why didn't you tell me any of this?"

"I hadn't told you she was making advances because I spoke with her and thought she'd stop. After she kissed me, I fully intended on telling you, but you had that emergency at the factory in China, and you were gone for a week. When you returned, we had the bullying situation to handle at the school with Elodie, and then Roan broke his arm mountain biking. By then, she was gone. The moment had passed, and I didn't think there was any point in upsetting you when I had handled it. You were under so much stress already, and I didn't want to add to your load. If I'd known you were there that night and you thought I was cheating, I would have told you everything then and there. I'm so sorry, babe. I hate you saw that. I hate you would even think I could do something like that to you." He clasps my face in his hands, kissing my tears away. "I love you, Rachel. I love you so fucking much, and I hate how things are between us. It's why I'm here today. I want to talk about us. About making changes that prioritize us as a couple and our family."

"I'm such an idiot." I sniffle, staring into his gorgeous

blue eyes. "I should have confronted you, and this all would have come out. The old me would have screamed and shouted at you, but I feel so lost these past six months, Brad. I don't feel like myself. I feel split down the middle all the time, and this isn't what I want for my life." I rest my hands on his chest. "I thought I was losing you." My voice cracks, and my tear ducts spring to life again. "I was so scared. It's felt like I've been dying inside. Every night we lie in bed beside one another with this massive gulf between us, and I'm silently crying and self-destructing. I thought you had no interest in me anymore, and instead of facing up to it, I have purposely forced it aside, afraid to confront it, because I wasn't ready to rip our family apart. I focused on work, using it as a distraction, denying the truth because I couldn't cope if it was true."

"It's going to be okay." His eyes probe mine. "Unless you don't love me anymore? Because that would change things." His expression turns somber.

"Brad, I love the fuck out of you. Always have. Always will. I thought you didn't love me."

"We can fix this. We *are* going to fix it. Together." His arms circle around me, and he pulls me into his body. I cling to him, closing my eyes and inhaling the familiar musky, spicy scent of his cologne and the feel of his toned body against mine. My muscles loosen up against him, and relief is a powerful relaxer.

"I have missed you," I say, and he eases back so he is looking me in the eyes.

"I have felt so empty without you. How did we let it get to this place?"

"I don't know."

"Just so we're clear, I'm not blaming you for any of this, Rach. I haven't been a good enough husband. I've been so focused on building my career, so I could adequately provide for you, that I neglected the truly important things. That you could think I would betray you shows how badly I have failed in proving my love to you."

"That's not all on you," I truthfully admit. "There is still a part of me, albeit small, that believes you settled for me. That I'm not the true love of your life."

Pain spreads across his face, and his distress is plain to see. Still, I don't regret admitting that truth. If we are to have any chance of salvaging our marriage and saving our family, there can be no more holding back. As much as I hate to hurt him, he needs to hear this. "I know you don't love Faye. I know, deep down, it's ridiculous to think that, but I can't help how I feel. When I thought you were having an affair, it brought all those old feelings to the surface. I felt like second best again."

"Hearing that kills me, but I'm glad you told me. I know it's not enough for me to say you are my entire world and I have never loved anyone the way I love you. I never loved Faye, and I sure as fuck did not settle for you. You saved me, Red." He plants a fierce kiss on my lips. "More than that, your love makes me whole. You complete me, and I'm going to prove it to you. I'm going to show you every day from now on through my actions. You are never going to doubt me or us ever again." Taking my hand, he holds it over his chest. "That's a promise."

A heaviness lifts from my chest as he urges me to

stand. His arms go around me, and we stand in the middle of my office, hugging and clinging to one another, and every second in his arms reassures me we can get through this. "We lost our way, but we'll rediscover our path."

"Damn fucking straight." Brad eases back, still keeping his arms around my back. "I love you, Rachel. You mean everything to me."

"I love you too," I say through blurry eyes.

We move at the same time, and a soothing warmth settles deep in my bones the instant our lips collide. Brad kisses me like we have all the time in the world, holding me like I'm precious cargo. Every glide of his lips against mine lifts another layer of stress from my shoulders, and I wish we were alone, that I could take him to bed and make love to him, because the need to reconnect in the most intimate way is riding me hard. I need to touch him and feel his touch. To remember how good we are together when we haven't lost sight of what's most important—each other.

"No more distance. No more not talking to one another. We turn over a new page, starting right now," he says, staring adoringly at me while tucking a piece of my hair behind my ear.

"I would really like that."

"I made a lunch reservation for us at Toscana. Why don't we talk more there and then head home early? Ky and Faye are taking the kids overnight."

"You spoke to him."

He nods. "I did. I wish I'd done it sooner. He helped kick my ass into gear. I should have taken action weeks ago. You needed me to man up, and I let you down, but I swear I won't let you down again."

"Let's agree not to blame one another. Yes, there are lessons we need to take from this, but we both chose not to communicate. To ignore what we both could see was happening. We let work take over every aspect of our lives. We know what's wrong, and we're committed to working together to fix it. Let's look forward, not back."

"My wife is so fucking smart and one of the most compassionate people I know," he says, melting my heart. He kisses the corner of my mouth. "She's also completely fucking gorgeous and sexy as sin. I'm as hot for her as I was the day I married her."

"She sounds like an amazing person."

"She truly is." He kisses me softly. "She's the most incredible woman I have ever met, and I'm so lucky to call her mine."

A wide grin spreads over my mouth. "My husband adores his family, and he works so hard to provide for us. He has a good heart, and he's pretty easy on the eyes too."

"Is that so?" Brad smirks as his hand moves lower, his fingers sweeping across my ass. "Should I be worried?"

I tighten my arms around his neck. "Not for a second. I only have eyes for you, and I love I get to call you mine."

"Grab your shit, and let's go."

I kiss him again. "I have missed kissing you. Missed making love to you. I have felt so lonely."

"Me too, but never again."

Brad puts my beautiful flowers in a vase of water while I fix my hair and makeup. Then I grab my bag, and we head out of my office, hand in hand. "I won't be back until Monday," I tell Majella as we pass through reception.

"Hold all calls unless it's an emergency," Brad adds, sliding his arm around my shoulders. "My wife deserves a well-earned break."

"That she does." Majella smiles at us. "Don't worry about a thing, Rachel. I will handle everything. Enjoy some time with your husband and those adorable kids of yours. I'll see you Monday."

The instant the elevator doors slide closed, Brad is on me, pushing me up against the wall and kissing me hard. His hands skim up and down my body, and it feels like I'm alive for the first time in months. I grab handfuls of his ass as we devour one another, and I'm giggling as we stumble out onto the pavement with swollen lips and matching cheesy grins.

We hold hands as we walk to the restaurant, stealing kisses and hugs, and it feels like I'm falling in love with my husband all over again.

We are seated at our usual table in the restaurant, at the back, and we quickly place our orders. I snuggle into my husband, and his arm automatically snakes around my shoulders, holding me close. "I have missed this kind of intimacy. It got to the point where I was nearly afraid to touch you."

"I was the same, and I'm going to make up for lost time." He leans in and kisses me. "I love kissing you, and I still get butterflies whenever you touch me."

"Ditto, babe," I say, beaming at the waiter as he pours wine into our glasses.

"I want to discuss something with you. It's to do with my job."

"Okay."

"I'm going to quit. I'm not loving it anymore, and we don't need the money. Our savings account is healthy, and your business is successful and growing fast. I thought I could stay home for a while. Look after the house and the kids and alleviate some of the pressure on you."

"Would you be happy doing that? You have worked so hard for your career."

"I have, and I wouldn't be giving it up. Just putting it on hold for a few years. You have sacrificed a lot for my career. Now it's my turn to put your needs and your career first. The kids won't stay kids forever. Spending more time with them won't be a chore, and if it eliminates some stress, meaning we have more quality time together as family and a couple, it's a no-brainer for me."

"Are you sure? I don't want you to do something that will make you unhappy."

"Supporting your dream makes me happy. Seeing you and the kids happy makes me happy."

"I love that, Brad, truly I do, but your needs matter too. Your happiness has to factor into it as well. I don't want you doing something you might end up regretting. I want you to be happy too."

"I'm unhappy now, Rach. Things need to change. I —" A shuddering sigh leaves his lips as he drags his free hand through his dark-blond hair.

"Say it, babe. No more hiding shit. Tell me what you were going to say."

"I miss the US. I miss my family and our friends. I want to move back home."

"Oh, thank God." I cup his shocked face. "We're on the same page, babe. I want to move back too."

"What about Jill and your dad and the office here?"

"I will appoint a director to run the office with Majella. Dad and Maggie are abroad on their adventures more than they are here, and he still has his apartment in New York. As for Jill, honestly, that friendship causes me additional stress. We're not close anymore, and I think I need to distance myself from her, at least for a while. There is nothing here stopping us from leaving."

I don't say that Jill found me at a weak moment and I confessed my fears to her. Or how she fed me a steady dose of hatred aimed in my husband's direction. If I'd told Faye, she would've immediately urged me to talk to Brad instead of supporting the view all men are cheating bastards and it must be true. I wanted to talk to Faye so badly, but it wouldn't have been right to involve her. I couldn't have asked her to keep it from Kyler. I didn't want our friends embroiled in our woes, and maybe that was partly due to the past too.

To be fair to Jill, I don't blame her for having that opinion after what Sam did. He cheated on her with one of their neighbors and knocked her up. Jill had been friends with the woman, pouring her heart out about the strain her failure to get pregnant was having on her marriage. That stupid bitch continued the friendship, providing a friendly ear while she was sleeping with her husband. How could any woman do that to another?

I understand Jill's devastation, and I hate what she

has endured. I have tried to be a good friend to her, but she doesn't make it easy. Faye thinks she's jealous of me and her sly digs are deep-seated envy. Faye has little to do with her anymore, and maybe I need to take a leaf out of her book.

Jill projected her bitterness onto me, and I think there's a part of her hoping my marriage ends and my family breaks up so she's not the only one going through what she's going through. I don't need that toxicity in my life, which is why I need some space. I won't permanently abandon her though. She's going through a really tough time, and I'm hopeful once she gets through this we can resume our usual friendship.

I don't blame Jill for what transpired between Brad and me, even if she gave me shitty advice. No, that's on me for not talking to my husband and choosing to believe the worst without giving him an opportunity to explain.

"You're not just saying that to appease me?" Brad asks, yanking me from my inner monologue.

I shake my head. "No. Not at all. We moved here for your job, and I thought we could make it work, but it's not. It nearly ended us. It's too stressful trying to run my business from here. I'm sick of traveling back and forth so much. I'm having issues with the management team in New York, and I need to be there more regularly. I miss Faye and the girls so much. I love Ireland, but the US is my home now."

"The kids are settled though."

"Kids adapt. They'll be fine. Maybe we could buy a place close to the Kennedys. The kids will be delighted to have all their friends close by. I can buy a helicopter and split my time between New York and working from home."

"We could buy a place with an Olympic-sized pool for Elodie, and Ky is talking about Cathal potentially starting motocross. Roan would love that too, and he's at the right age to start."

Excitement sparkles in his eyes as we stare at one another. "Sounds like a plan." He kisses me quickly, just before the waiter arrives with our food. He places heaped plates of pasta in front of us and tops up our drinks before departing.

"How soon do you want to move?" he asks, picking up his fork.

"As soon as we can make it happen. Preferably before the kids return to school. Faye could vouch for us at the school her kids attend, and I know they'd let us stay with them until we find a place." Their house is massive with plenty of spare bedrooms, so it's not like we'd be living in each other's pockets either.

"I'll talk to Kade in the morning and contact the moving company."

A heady warmth pervades every part of my body. "This already feels so right," I admit, twirling a forkful of spaghetti against my spoon.

"It does." He nuzzles my nose and whispers in my ear. "Now all that's left to do is finish up here so I can take my beautiful wife home and make love to her all afternoon."

Chapter Nine
Kaden

I get off the phone with Brad, lean back in my chair, and sigh. Fuck. His timing couldn't be worse, but I can't fault him for the decision he's made. He's right to prioritize his marriage and his family. I stifle a yawn as I stand, stretching my arms up over my head. It's early, and I slept like shit last night, thanks to Milly and her boy drama.

Walking to the floor-to-ceiling window, which runs the length of the back of my home office, I stand in front of the glass, staring at the rain tumbling in heavy sheets from the sky. It's not unusual to have rain showers in August, but this kind of torrential rain is rare. It pitter-patters against the window as I survey the gorgeous grounds at the rear of our new house. Eva planted most of the flowerbeds and shrubs herself, and it's an impressive feat. Every night, we walk hand in hand through the gardens, and it's one of my favorite things to do.

We moved sixteen months ago to be closer to the fam. Everyone else lives in the vicinity, and all of us are about three or four miles from one another. I love that my kids are close to their cousins, and they get to spend plenty of time with their grandparents. My parents are both retired, and in between traveling, they love babysitting their grandkids.

One of the reasons we bought this place is for the three-bedroom bungalow on the grounds. This house used to be a boutique hotel, but the previous owners completely gutted and renovated it ten years ago. The bungalow was built for the hotel owner's personal use, and it's a decent-sized house.

Eva's Dad turns seventy next year, and while he's still in good health, the two-year stint he did in jail—for financial fraud and money laundering for Eva's psychotic criminal now-dead first husband—worked him over hard. Eva was worrying constantly about him. We offered to buy him a place so he could move out of that dingy one-bed condo he was living in, but he's a stubborn, proud old man, and he refused. It wasn't as easy when we bought a place that came with a separate house just sitting there unused.

Matthew is very close to his Granddad Jack, and they go fishing every Saturday morning at Lake Waban. Sometimes, he stays overnight at the bungalow to keep his granddad company. Eva loves how close the two of them are.

Rubbing the back of my neck, I head out of my office in the direction of the kitchen. The radio is on, and my wife is singing along as she makes waffles for the kids.

I creep up on Eva on tiptoe, sliding my arms around her curvy waist from behind, as she drops a couple of waffles onto a stacked plate. She shrieks, and I chuckle, nipping her earlobe with my teeth. "You make it too easy."

"You are going to give me a coronary one of these days, Kade." She leans her back against my chest, angling her head and looking up at me. "Morning, darling." Her loving smile ghosts over my face, and contentment flows through my veins.

"Morning, beautiful." I lean down and kiss her voluptuous lips, still getting a kick out of the fact she's mine and I can do this whenever I want. "I love you," I add because I make it a point to tell her at least once a day. I know what it's like to love her and not be able to tell her, and I never want to experience that again.

"I love you too, boytoy." She turns in my arms and cheekily pats my ass. "If the kids weren't due to appear any moment, I'd drag your sexy ass back to bed and have my wicked way with you."

Apparently, women hit their sexual prime in their late thirties to early forties, and from the way Eva's been jumping my bones any chance she gets lately, I'd say it's true. My wife turned forty-three this year, and she is still so fucking beautiful. In fact, I'd say she's even more beautiful than when I first met her, and I don't say that lightly because Eva was a complete knockout in her twenties.

"Forget the bed." I squeeze her boob through her silk robe. "The laundry room is right there." I waggle my brows suggestively, and I'm contemplating throwing her over my shoulder when Milly walks into the kitchen.

"You two are gross." She makes a face as she hops up onto a stool at the island unit.

"I hope you're as lucky as us to find someone you love with every fiber of your being," Eva says, sliding out from my arms.

"You don't really mean that," Milly retorts, and I brace myself for it.

Eva carries the plate of waffles over to the counter and sets it down in front of our only daughter. Bowls of fruit salad, compote, and yogurt are already laid out, and Milly helps herself to some fruit along with a couple of waffles.

She inherited my height—both our kids are tall for their age—and her mother's stunning facial features. I barely see any of myself when I look at her, and I'm loath to claim her attitude as my own, but I can't deny I was a little shit at her age too.

"If you did, you'd have no issue with me dating Justin," she adds, glaring at me as she shoves a spoonful of fruit in her mouth.

"I have no issue with you dating Justin when you're thirty," I deadpan, pouring three glasses of freshly squeezed orange juice.

"Kade." Eva pins whiskey-colored eyes on me, her look warning me not to go there again. I feign innocence and clamp my lips shut because I don't want to argue with my daughter before she leaves for horse riding.

"What your father means is we are okay with you dating Justin when you are seventeen."

I almost choke on my juice. I never fucking agreed to that! Justin will still be four years older, and I don't want my sweet seventeen-year-old dating a twenty-one-year-old horndog any more than I want my sweet fourteen-year-old dating an eighteen-year-old horndog.

Eva whips her head to me, narrowing her eyes and cautioning me to shut the fuck up. I stuff a waffle in my mouth because I don't trust myself not to speak. We can have this out after Milly leaves.

"I don't see what the problem is. You're five years older than Dad. If it's okay for you, how is it not okay for me?"

"That's not the problem, and you know it," I say, purposely not looking at my wife. I can't fucking stay quiet a second longer. "He's too old for you *now*. There is a vast difference between fourteen and eighteen, between a freshman and a senior. I know how teenage boys think. Trust me when I tell you that boy has only one thing on his mind, and if he lays one finger on you, I'll beat the—"

My words are muffled, my sentence cut off, when my wife slaps her hand over my mouth.

"I think it's best we continue this conversation later," Eva says, in a calm tone, as if our daughter currently doesn't have steam billowing from her ears and venom ready to pour from her mouth. "Elaine's mom will be here in five minutes. Finish your breakfast, and we'll talk when you get home."

"I've lost my appetite." Milly glares at me as Eva withdraws her hand from my mouth.

"This is coming from a place of love," I remind my daughter as she stomps away.

"Could've fooled me," she yells over her shoulder

before exiting the kitchen and slamming the door behind her.

"You just had to go there." Eva shakes her head, setting a plate down in front of me.

"It needs to be repeated until she sees sense." I load waffles and fruit onto my plate.

"She's a hormonal teenager. She's not going to see sense."

"Not helping," I growl before swallowing a mouthful of juice. "Why couldn't she stay young and sweet and innocent forever?"

Eva's features soften as she wraps her arms around me. "We can't stop her from growing up or from dating, but we do need to set some ground rules."

"He's too old. It's not happening."

"I agree, but the more we deny her, the harder she'll rebel. We need to get creative."

"So, what?" My fork clangs on the marble countertop as it drops from my hand. "We just let her date that little perv and say nothing when he steals her virtue and breaks her heart?"

Eva rolls her eyes as she climbs onto the stool alongside me. "I swear to God, Kade. You and your brothers have such a flair for the dramatic."

"If you grew up in my house, you'd be a bit of a drama queen too."

"What the what?" Matthew says, strolling into the kitchen with a puckered brow. He's only wearing pajama bottoms and a sleepy smile. His dark hair is sticking up in all directions and he's yawning like he hasn't just slept nine hours straight. "Did you just call yourself a drama queen?" he asks, grabbing a waffle and taking a large bite out of it.

"Your father was giving your sister a run for her money just now."

"You can't let her date Justin." He walks to the refrigerator and removes the jug of juice. "He only wants one thing."

"Thank you." I slam my hands down on the counter and level a look at Eva.

"I didn't say you were wrong," Eva says, slanting me with a look of her own. "Only that your current reaction is not helping. All you are doing is encouraging her to dig her heels in and date him behind our backs. Then we have no way of knowing what she is doing or where she is going."

"Mom's right, Dad," Matthew says, hopping up onto the stool across from me.

"I thought you were on my side."

"I am, but you know how stubborn Milly is. I'm not even sure she likes him that much. You're making this into a challenge."

"So, what should we do?"

"Tell her she can go on a date with him, but you have to approve the location. Give her an early curfew, and say he has to pick her up from the house. Scare the shit out of him, Dad, so he's afraid to lay a finger on her. Ask Hewson and his buddies to go wherever they are and watch from a distance. That way, if Justin tries anything, Hewson can get involved. Milly knows you'll be tracking her on the app, so she won't lie."

Eva and I stare at our son with our mouths hanging

open in shocked awe. It's so hard to believe he's thirteen sometimes. Cathal may be a savant, but our son is wise and intelligent, and he makes me so fucking proud.

"That's a pretty impressive plan. Do you think it'll work?" I ask.

"Milly thinks she's more grown up than she is, but she's smart, and she's not reckless. You need to trust her. She's not going to let Justin take something she's not prepared to give him. I'm guessing either she'll grow sick of him pretty quick, or he'll give up when she doesn't give it up."

"Jesus." I almost choke on my tongue. I can't bear thinking about my little girl having sex. I feel ill thinking it.

This parenting lark is not easy, and raising teenagers is a freaking minefield.

"Thanks for the suggestion. We'll consider it," Eva says, ever the voice of reason.

"You need to look out for your sister," I add.

"Duh, Dad. Of course. I know you don't want to hear this, but Milly gets a lot of attention from the boys at school. It's not surprising. She's gorgeous, just like Mom."

"That is true." I slide my arm around Eva's waist, pulling her in for a quick kiss. "It's all your fault for passing such stunning genes to our little girl," I tease though it's no lie. Milly is Eva's mini-me, in the same way Matthew is mine.

Matthew grabs another waffle and slides off the stool. "I'm meeting the guys for a game in a half hour. Can one of you give me a ride?"

"I'll drive you," Eva says.

"Cool. Thanks, Mom."

We watch him stroll out of the kitchen, all long gangly legs and skinny arms. He shot up this summer, and the rest of his body has yet to catch up.

"I can't believe we're taking advice from a thirteen-year-old," I say as Eva gets up to pour two coffees.

"Matthew is a wise, old soul in a young body."

"Isn't that the truth." I accept a mug of coffee from my wife. "Thanks, darling."

"Let's just think about it today, and we can talk later and make a decision then."

"Fine. Oh, I almost forgot to tell you. Brad just resigned."

Eva's mouth drops open. "What?" she splutters.

"I know. He caught me off guard too." I tell her what Brad told me about his priorities and how he came to this decision.

"This is a blow, but I don't fault Brad for putting his family first. I feel bad we may have contributed to the situation. We never should have asked him to relocate overseas."

"Hey, that's not on us. He could have said no. He knows we would never have fired him."

"True, but I feel some responsibility. He's family."

"They'll be fine. Everything will work out." I smooth my hand up and down her back. "He said he'll work remotely until we find a replacement, and he offered to contact a recruitment agency in Dublin if we want to start the process ASAP."

"I don't know." Eva props a shapely hip against the counter as she stares off into space. "Maybe this is an opportunity to reshape things. Brad has done a fantastic job and shown the potential in the European market. Maybe it's time we target the market more aggressively. Hire someone in the UK and a couple of key European destinations and really go after those areas. If we hire local, it keeps the traveling to a minimum, ensuring we don't face this again in a year or two's time."

"That's a smart plan, and we have the market research data to back it up. We could also consider advertising the position within the sales team here. We have some talented individuals working for us who might be interested in the promotion. At the very least, we should look for someone internally to help with the recruitment and getting these new hires trained."

She bobs her head. "We should head to the office tomorrow and talk to Gavin and Gina. Get this process up and running."

"Sounds like a plan. I'll call Gina now and get it on the calendar." The stool screeches as I get up.

"Make it early," Eva says, placing her small hand on my arm. "We have guests coming tomorrow night."

"We do?" This is the first I'm hearing of it.

"Presley and Kent are coming over."

"What have you done?"

"It's time, Kade." Eva circles her arms around my waist and peers up at me. "Presley and I are staging an intervention. If we leave it up to you two, you'll never reconcile."

"We talk," I protest, hating to be forced into doing anything.

"You say the bare minimum at family events. That is not talking."

"He made his feelings clear, and I don't blame him. I let him down, and I don't know how I can ever make it right."

"That was almost eight years ago. It's time to let it go. You're both hurting, and you need to just sit down and talk it all out. I know you miss him, and I know he misses you. You're both as stubborn as each other, so we're not taking no for an answer this time."

The girls have tried to resolve this before. Eva isn't as close to Kent as she once was, because we're all busy with family life, but she still talks to him more than my other brothers. She usually broaches the subject with me once a year, and I have no doubt she's mentioned it to Kent too. I'm not sure if there is anything left to be said, but I should try. I didn't do right by him, and continuing to let the years roll by without making an effort to fix things isn't right either. "Okay."

"Yeah?" Her eyes light up with hope.

I nod, holding her close as I consider how lucky I am to have such a compassionate, caring woman for my wife. "I miss my brother, and it has gone on long enough. I will do my best to make things right."

Chapter Ten
Eva

K ade nuzzles my neck as I wake, his muscular arm sliding around my waist from behind. "Good morning, darling."

Feeling his long, thick erection pressing against my lower back, I rub up against him as I murmur, "It *is* a good morning, and I know exactly how we can make it even better."

"I like where your mind has gone." Kade moves his hand up my body to cup a breast.

"Hold that thought," I say, angling my head and pressing a kiss to the underside of his prickly jawline. "I need to pee and brush my teeth." I hop up and race to the bathroom the same time he does. After we attend to business, we crawl back into bed to pick up where we left off.

"I'm so glad we went into the office yesterday afternoon." Kade nips at my earlobe as he tugs on the hem of my silk nightie. "This is a much more productive way to spend our morning."

"I'm glad you think so." I flash him a saucy wink as I

sit up, pulling my nightdress over my head and tossing it aside. "Your turn." I whip the covers off and yank his light cotton sleep pants down.

"Someone is feisty." He grins, folding his arms behind his head, as I straddle his thighs.

"Is being hot for my husband a crime?"

"Fuck no," he hisses as I lower myself over his big dick. "I love how insatiable you are lately."

I hold still on top of him and close my eyes, savoring the feel of his body pulsing inside mine. My eyes blink open. "I love you." I bend down and kiss him. Kade quickly takes control, hardening the kiss as he clasps my head and devours my mouth while I sit on top of him, neither of us moving.

"Thank you for sharing your life with me," he says when we break our lip-lock. "I never take it, or you, for granted."

"I know you don't. Neither of us do after what we endured to get to this point."

"I never forget it," he adds, moving his fingers to where we are joined. His thumb presses gently on my clit as I start to rock on top of him. "Ride your cock, darling. Take what you need."

I bounce up and down on him for a while, both of us moaning and whimpering until Kade flips us over, automatically knowing when I need it harder and faster. My husband fucks me with devoted expertise, caressing every inch of my skin as he simultaneously drives in and out of me with deep, hard thrusts.

We come together before collapsing on the bed, bodies sated and chests heaving in the aftermath of our lovemaking. Kade curls an arm around my waist, pulling me in close to his side. He dusts kisses all over my face. "Sometimes, I miss you even when you're right next to me because the intensity of the way I feel about you is such that I can't ever bear to be parted. Even when you're with me."

"I know what you mean." I trail my fingers through the dark hair covering his chest. "No one else I know spends so much time with their significant other. I love how much we genuinely crave and enjoy time together." Kade and I rarely have arguments. I'm sure marriage counselors would have something to say about that, like some level of arguing is healthy, but we don't. And we spend a lot of time together, working our business, running the house, and looking after the kids.

That's not to imply we don't have our own interests, separate friends, and occasions where we are apart because all of that happens. But I genuinely adore my husband. He's my best friend, my lover, my family, my partner in life.

"Loving you is as easy as breathing," my husband says, tenderly kissing my mouth. "I never knew life could be this good."

I twist on my side and prop up on one elbow, peering down at my handsome husband. "You're an amazing husband and father, Kade. We're lucky to have you."

Kade gently clasps my chin, pulling my face to his. His lips brush softly against mine, and my heart swoons. "As much as I want to stay here all day, we should probably get up and break the good news to our daughter."

After talking it through last night, we have decided to go with Matthew's suggestion.

"Yes." I rest my head on his chest. One of my favorite things to do is listen to his heart beat. I will never forget the sheer terror I felt that day in the warehouse when he got shot. His blood was all over me, and I was terrified I'd lost him. I slide my arm around his body and wrap my leg around his, clinging to him to remember he's here and he's whole. Hearing Kade's heart beating steadily under my ear is like music to my ears. It always reminds me of how close he came to death and how strong and vibrant he is.

"Do you need me to get anything for tonight?" he asks as we reluctantly separate and get out of bed.

"Could you go to the Italian deli and pick up some ladyfingers? I haven't made tiramisu for Kent in a long time."

"Sure," he says, heading for the bathroom.

"Kade." I call out to him as I slip my robe on and slide my feet into my matching slippers. "How are you feeling about tonight?"

"A little anxious, but I'm glad you arranged it. I want to repair my relationship with my brother."

I walk toward him and hug him. "That makes me happy, and he wants that too."

Kade tips my chin up. "He has said that?"

"Not outwardly, but I can tell. And Presley said it's true."

A sigh heaves from his lips. "Good. It's time to let the past stay in the past."

"I dropped by my parents' place on the way back from the deli," Kade says later that night as I'm putting the finishing touches to the dinner. "Hewson was there with Kalvin, so I mentioned Milly's date, and he said he'd watch out for her."

"He's a good kid."

"He is though Kal says they are still having issues with him sneaking out to party and meet girls."

I can't contain my grin. "Karma is whooping his ass!"

"For sure," my husband says, setting the kitchen table. We have decided to eat in here rather than the formal dining room as it's more casual. Plus, the large kitchen-slash-family room faces the rear of our property, and at night, the stunning views of the garden are beautiful to look at with the backdrop of the moon and stars. "But I seriously doubt Hewson is half as wild as his father was."

"Everything worked out for Kal, and I'm sure it will for Hewson too," I say, grating chocolate over the top of the tiramisu before putting it in the fridge.

The doorbell chimes, and Kade stiffens a little. "Relax, it's the pizza delivery guy. They won't be here for a while yet." The kids are having pizza and watching movies in our home theater while we share dinner with Presley and Kent. "Everything is prepared. I'm going to grab a shower and get changed. I'll get the pizza on the way."

When I return forty minutes later, Kade has the table

set and the bottle of red wine airing. He bought some nonalcoholic beer for Kent as he's most likely the designated driver. Kent enjoys a beer, now and again, but he tends not to push it these days. He's completely clean of drugs, and he doesn't touch them, knowing it's a slippery slope. He was never addicted in the traditional sense, confining his drug use to the weekends, but it's better he's completely weaned off them now.

Kade is wearing a pristine white dress shirt and black pants, having changed while I was showering, and he looks classically handsome, if a bit tense. I drop down on the couch beside him and throw my arms around his shoulders. "It'll be fine. He wants this reconciliation as much as you do."

The doorbell chimes for the second time in an hour, and I know it's our guests. "I'll go," Kade says, getting up the same time I do.

"We'll greet them together," I add, slipping my hand in his. "A united front, like always."

Chapter Eleven
Kent

I'm sweating buckets as I stand outside Kaden and Eva's house, waiting for the door to open. Which is stupid. He's my brother, and it's not like I'm going in front of the firing line. Still, we haven't uttered more than passing comments to one another in years. This is the first time the four of us are spending time alone, without the buffer of family, and I'm nervous.

"Breathe, baby." Presley smooths a hand up and down my back. "Everything is going to be fine. You'll see."

The door opens, ending my chance to make a run for it.

"You guys look great," Eva says, her warm, welcoming smile doing little to settle my nerves.

"We're happy you could make it," Kade adds, and they step aside to let us inside their stunning home.

"Thanks for inviting us," Presley says, hugging our sister-in-law.

Kade and I stand awkwardly in the hallway while the

girls embrace. Fuck it. If things are to change, it starts now. I lean in and slap him on the back, relieved when he returns the gesture.

The girls are wearing matching giddy grins when we break apart, and I roll my eyes as I lean in and kiss Eva on the cheek. "If you made tiramisu, I'll love you forever."

"I thought love came with no conditions. That it's something you give freely," she coyly replies, and if she was mine, I'd take her over my knee and slap her ass for her sassiness.

"It is, and stop stirring the pot." I glance at Kade. "We're grown-ass men. We can resolve our own differences."

"I never suggested you couldn't." Eva loops her arm in mine, dragging me into the kitchen. "I thought we'd eat in here. It's more relaxing."

"That's cool. I love this room."

"Oh, shoot," Presley says, and I snicker. She has taken to saying that lately to avoid cursing in front of our precocious daughter. "We left the flowers and champagne in the trunk."

"Give me your keys, and I'll get them," Kade offers, holding out his hand.

"I'll come with," I say, preferring to get this conversation over and done with now. Dinner will be strained otherwise.

The girls trade looks. They're as subtle as a brick, but I can't blame them. This shit has gone on long enough, and it's put both of them in awkward positions at times.

We walk out of the room in tense silence until Kade

breaks it in the hall. "Congrats on your promotion. You must be thrilled."

I shrug as we walk toward the front door. "As long as I get to continue the work I'm doing with disadvantaged kids, I don't really care."

"It's nice to be recognized," he says, opening the door and stepping outside.

"It is. The company has been good to me. I like working there, and they have a lot of family-friendly policies, which means I can fit things around Pres's schedule."

Our feet crunch on gravel as we walk toward our car. "It makes me happy to see you happy." He props a hip against the side of my Lexus when we reach it.

"Does it?"

"Yes," he says without hesitation. "I'm proud of you, Kent. You're the strongest of all of us."

"I wouldn't say that, but I am proud of how far I have come." I lean my back against the passenger side window. "There was a time I didn't think I'd make it. It was the first year after the assault when I barely had the will to survive."

"I hate you went through that alone. I hate I didn't notice."

"You weren't there in the aftermath. You were hiding in the city, licking your wounds after Mom and Dad dropped the bomb on you. I get it."

"I'm your eldest brother. I should have been there for you. I shouldn't have been so caught up in my own problems that you didn't feel like you could come to me."

I shrug, not wanting to delve too deep into old

ground. I know we need to clear the air, but I don't want to rehash every painful part of our past. I turn and eyeball him. "If you could turn back time, what would you do differently?"

"Everything. I would have been there for all of you more. I didn't just fail you, Kent. I neglected Ky and Kalvin, Keanu and Keaton too."

"We weren't your responsibility, Kade. You weren't our parents."

"I know that, but I still shouldn't have neglected my brothers. That's not my biggest regret though." He maintains eye contact as he talks. "I wrote you off as a trouble-maker. I never stopped to consider there was anything driving your behavior. You'd always been a rebel, and I saw it as you refusing to grow up. I was narrow-minded and judgmental in a way I'm not with others. You are my brother. I should have cut you some slack. I should have listened to my wife when she said there was something weighing on your mind. Also, if I'm honest, I can admit I was a little bit jealous of how close you and Eva became. It served to highlight how distant we were."

My eyes pop wide because that surprises the shit out of me. "You never gave any indication it bothered you."

"Because it didn't. Not for more than a fleeting minute." He leans against the side of the car, crossing one ankle over the other. "I don't begrudge your relationship. Not at all. I was jealous she could talk to you in a way I couldn't, but I was glad you had her to talk to. I didn't see it at the time, but it made me realize what a piece-of-shit brother I was to you. I always believed your self-destructive behavior was completely selfish and a desire to be the center of attention. I saw how much it upset Mom. You caused arguments at family events, and I know you often did that on purpose to stir shit. It was hard to be around you sometimes, Kent, even if you're my brother and I have always loved you. It was easier to think the worst and not trust you. I didn't see your pain because it was hidden behind your troublesome behavior. That is what drove me to react as I did."

"That makes sense."

"It does?"

"Yeah." I know I was a prick to be around at times, and I did stir trouble on purpose.

"I hate that I closed myself off to you," he continues. "I hate that I wasn't with our brothers at the warehouse the night they found you. God, Kent." His voice cracks, and tears well in his eyes. "You died. You fucking *died*, and I wasn't there. As long as I live, I will never forgive myself for that." His chest heaves as he pauses for a second. Emotion bleeds into the air. "I truly am sorry, Kent. For everything, and if I could go back, I would redo all of that."

Sincerity radiates from his eyes, and it's etched all over his face. I hear the regret in his voice, and this is the most honest conversation we've had in years. "There is so much I wish I could do over, but there is no point in looking back. We were young. We all made mistakes." I wet my lips as I stare at my brother. "I want to move past this. It's time." I pause for a split second. "I forgive you, brother."

He stares at me in shock, blinking profusely for a few seconds. "How?"

"Holding on to a grudge is childish and petty. I'm in a good place in my life. So are you. It's time to bury the hatchet."

"But you were so angry with me, and rightly so," Kade replies. "I let you down in the worst way. How can you forgive me?"

"I was hurting badly back then, Kade. I lashed out at everyone because I wanted you all to hurt too. The truth is, I am far from blameless. I should have spoken up. I should have confided in Keats and Keanu. I had my reasons, but I chose not to say anything, and it's not fair to expect you all to be mind readers. Yes, I'm disappointed none of you saw how troubled I was or did anything about it, but everyone was dealing with shit, and shit happens."

"You're a good man, Kent. I'm not sure I'd be so charitable in your shoes."

"You would because continuing to let this come between us means my abusers are still winning." I straighten up. "They took enough from me. It ends completely right now. You're my brother. I love you." I almost choke over the lump wedged in my throat. "And I choose to forgive you."

Kade grabs me into a hug, and my arms go around him. "I love you too," he says. His body trembles as much as mine, which is how I know he is feeling this as deeply as I am. We hug it out for a few minutes, like a couple of pussies, and I just know the women have their noses pressed to the window, watching this go down. When we break apart, we're both clearly emotional. "I'm not worthy of your forgiveness"—Kade clamps a hand on my shoulder—"but I will accept it if you can accept my apology for failing you. I promise I won't let you down again. If you need me, for anything, I'm here for you."

"Thanks, man. That means a lot."

"So, we're good?"

"We're good."

We grin at each other for a few seconds, like idiots, and the last bit of tension that was clinging to me from the past flutters away in the light summertime breeze.

"Come on." Kade squeezes my shoulder as I pop the trunk on the car. "We'd better head inside. Eva probably has dinner ready to be served."

Chapter Twelve
Presley

"**I** want a tattoo." Shania pouts as she climbs into her booster seat in the back of my SUV. "It's not fair. Daddy already has squillions. I want *one*. Just one teeny tiny tattoo." Her gaze bounces between Kent and me. "No one will know. You can hide it where nobody will see it." Her eyes widen as if a light bulb has just gone off in her head. She bounces on her seat. "I'll get Eliot's name on my hip, like you have Dad's on yours! Then we'll match, Mom!"

Kent smothers his laughter with a fake cough.

She places her palms together, lifting her joined hands up and pinning us with doe eyes. "Puh-lease, Mommy. Puh-lease, Daddy."

I exchange a knowing look with my husband over the hood of the car before sliding behind the wheel. This is Shania's most persistent argument, but she's particularly frustrated today because Kent stupidly let it slip he's coming by the studio, later on, for more ink. "If no one will see it, what is the point?" I ask, glancing back at her as I power up the engine.

"*I'll know*. That's the point." Her lower lip juts out as she eyeballs me with stubborn determination. God help us when she's a teenager. I already know she's going to give us hell. I see what Lana and Kalvin are going through with Hewson. Milly is putting Kade and Eva through the wringer over boys and dating, and Faye and Kyler and Brad and Rachel are all dealing with tween hormones and attitudes. Fun times ahead!

Kent chuckles as he closes the door to the back seat, popping his head through the open window. "If you want a tattoo when you're eighteen, you can have one. Hundreds of them, if you like. But until then, it's temporary tattoos for my princess." He tweaks her nose, and she angrily swats his hand away.

"It's not fair. Uncle Austen said Eliot can have a tattoo when he's sixteen."

"That's not true." I eye my daughter through the mirror. "Eliot will have to wait until he's eighteen too." Eliot has a vivid imagination and fanciful notions. I am pretty sure he's the one who put this idea in our seven-year-old's head. I know for a fact that Austen and Keaton have had similar conversations with their son. It's kind of funny when you consider Austen started getting tattoos at sixteen. I'm sure, when it comes down to it, if the kids are mature enough and they want ink at sixteen or seventeen, we'll most likely relent, but it would be unwise to mention that now.

The four of us have agreed this is the party line, and we're sticking to it.

"Tattoos are for grown-ups, and you are still my li'l princess. Enjoy being a kid, and stop trying to grow up too fast," Kent says, leaning in to kiss her cheek. She tries to pull away, but he's not having it, holding her face in his large palms and pressing a succession of wet kisses all over her face.

"Daddy, stop!" She giggles, incapable of staying mad at him for long. "You're slobbering all over me like a dog!"

Oh no. Here we go.

"If I can't have a tattoo, can I have a dog?"

"We told you we're thinking about that." Kent semi-lies because we have already decided to buy her a puppy for her next birthday.

"You need to prove you can be a really good girl if you want a puppy. They are a big responsibility," I say.

"I'm responsible." She sits up straighter. "I'll do all the work. You and Daddy won't have to do a thing!"

Yeah right. I know exactly how this will go down. But I don't mind. We have a large garden on the grounds of our ginormous house, money to take care of a dog, and plenty of love to go around.

Kent smiles adoringly at her. Shania has him wrapped around her little finger, and the two of them are thick as thieves. Tears prick the backs of my eyes, like always, when I watch my husband with our daughter. Their heads are pressed together now, and they're whispering secrets.

I wish we had been able to conceive again, but it hasn't happened. At least not yet. With my issues, it's a miracle I got pregnant with Shania at all, and I count my blessings. We don't use contraception, and I'm only thirty-five, so it could still happen. We have discussed adoption too, and if I don't conceive in the next year or two, we will probably pursue that avenue.

Or maybe surrogacy, like Austen and Keaton did with Lia.

"Okay, Daddy needs to leave, or he'll be late for work." Nuzzling his nose into Shania's dark hair, Kent dusts kisses over her head before stepping away from the window. "Have a good day at Nanny and Grandad's. Love you, princess."

"Love you, Daddy. To the moon and back." Shania blows kisses, and Kent pretends to catch them. I press the button to close Shania's window as I lower mine.

Kent rounds the car, sticking his head through my window to kiss me. It's our usual morning routine. Closing my eyes, I wrap my arms around my sexy husband's neck as he kisses me, thrusting his tongue into my mouth and devouring me. He's shameless, but I adore how affectionate he is. He is always kissing me, holding my hand, putting his arm around my shoulders, or squeezing my ass.

Reluctantly, we tear our lips apart. "I'll call you when I'm leaving the office later. Do my parents know we'll be late picking the princess up tonight?"

"They know, and they're cool with it. Alex said Shania could sleep over if we want."

A devilish glint gleams in Kent's eye. "I'm surprised you didn't agree on the spot." Darting in, he nibbles on my earlobe and whispers, "Think of all the naughty things I can do to you if we have a free house, Presley baby."

I squirm on my seat as liquid lust pools low in my body. "God, you turn me on so much with just the promise of your cock," I whisper. "That is a true talent."

"Arrange the sleepover, sweetheart." He pecks my lips. "I'm going to make you scream my name all night long."

The last client leaves, and I flip the sign on the door to closed and lock the door. Kent is already en route here from the law firm he works at, so I have a few minutes to prepare my workstation and make myself presentable. I grab a quick shower in the staff bathroom, keeping my hair out of the water, and get changed into a tight-fitting black dress and my lace-up knee-high boots. Pulling my hair into a high ponytail, I slick red lipstick on my lips and apply some mascara before spritzing perfume on my neck and wrists. Then I call a local steak and seafood restaurant and make a reservation for later while I clean my work area and wait for my husband to arrive.

"You look fucking gorgeous," Kent says when I let him into the building Austen and I co-own. We use the main retail space for Tenley Ink and rent the adjoining smaller units to a couple of other businesses. The over-head apartments are rented to private individuals. He reels me into his arms, slapping my ass, as he rocks his hips into mine. "Smell fucking gorgeous too," he adds, running his nose along the exposed column of my neck.

"I could say the same about you," I admit, shucking

out of his embrace and threading my fingers in his. "You are hot as fuck in that suit." He's wearing a navy Hugo Boss two-piece with a pristine white dress shirt and a silver and navy tie. Glimmering silver cuff links sparkle under the bright lights of the studio as I lead him to my work area at the back. All the blinds are pulled down at the front, and everyone else has left for the day, so we have complete privacy. I have some ideas what we can do with it, and I'm not talking about the lion design I'm planning on inking on Kent's lower back.

"I need you, Presley baby," Kent says, slamming me up against the wall when we step into my room. "I am so horny for you."

"Great minds think alike," I rasp, whimpering as his fingers creep under the hem of my dress. "I have been thinking about sex with you all day."

"Do you think every married couple is like this?" he asks, dotting open-mouthed kisses along my neck and my collarbone as his wicked fingers continue their upward trajectory under my dress.

"Hot for one another?" I inquire, arching a brow.

"Yes." His lips tease the corner of my mouth.

"I think we're bucking the norm, but I'm no expert." A squeal escapes my lips when his fingers brush the front of my panties.

"I think we're so fucking lucky, Pres." Lifting his head, he stalls his fingers, much to my disappointment. "We have a great marriage. We're a real team. We confide in one another and enjoy being together. Our daughter is incredible, and our sex life blows my fucking mind. Life couldn't get any better."

"Romantic Kent still has the power to sucker punch me in the ovaries." I clasp his gorgeous face in my hands. "I love you so much, and I love our life. I didn't know it was possible to be this happy."

"Me either." He leans in and kisses me tenderly while his fingers make slow circles on the outside front of my panties. "We're living the dream, babe."

"We are, but you know what would make it even better?"

He flashes me a cocky smile, showcasing a set of perfect white teeth. "Me fucking you over the tattoo table?"

"You read my mind." I gasp when his fingers slide under the lace and he parts my folds.

"Fuck, babe. You're dripping."

"I told you I've been dreaming about this all day."

"You're my every fantasy come to life, Pres. I hope you realize that." I shudder with desire when he slides two fingers inside me.

"As you are mine. Now fuck me, husband. You promised I'd be screaming your name all night. I think it's time we got started."

Chapter Thirteen
Austen

"Hello?" I tentatively call out when Colton and I step through the door of Tenley Ink, greeted by the distinct sound of moaning. Colton grins as I slam to a halt, wondering if I can sneak back out before Presley and Kent notice. I knew she was adding new ink to his back tonight, and when I dropped Eliot and Lia at my in-laws house an hour ago, Alex mentioned she was taking Shania overnight too so Kent and Pres could have a night out. I had already made plans with my buddy to go for drinks and I thought they might like to join us.

Seems they had other plans in mind, and now we're intruding.

I turn to Colton. "Think we can sneak out without them noticing?" I ask just as Presley emits a loud scream.

"Damn! Is he fucking her or killing her?" he asks over a chuckle.

"Kent doesn't do anything by half. We have shared

accommodations with them before, and trust me when I say they are *loud* in the bedroom."

"Let's go. Leave them to their fun." Colton raises one shoulder, and we creep back out the way we came in. I lock the door behind me, and we set out on foot to the sports bar two blocks away.

"So, how are things?" I ask. "Have you adjusted to the gaping hole in your life yet?" Colton retired from the NFL six weeks ago by choice, but that doesn't mean it's easy to adapt when football has been your life for so long. I speak from experience. Injury forced me to retire two years ago, and I still miss it so much. Not the training or the early morning starts but the camaraderie in the locker room, my teammates, and game day. It's like I have lost a limb.

"It's so weird waking up every day without a schedule. Even though I don't set my alarm until eight, my eyes open at five a.m. on the dot every morning."

"It took me months to adjust my sleeping routine," I admit as we walk. "I'm still an early riser, but I don't miss the super early starts."

"What do you miss?" he asks, pushing through the double-fronted glass doors into the bar. We're immediately accosted with a multitude of sounds and smells. There's a preseason exhibition game on the TV, and while they feast on wings, burgers, fries, and pizza, drunk patrons are hollering as the 49ers score a touchdown against the Buccaneers.

"Having a purpose," I truthfully admit, instantly feeling guilty.

"That sounds serious," my buddy says as a waitress

escorts us to an empty booth at the back of the bar I reserved in advance. We can still see the TV from here, but it will be quieter, which is good. Because I really need my buddy's advice. And I don't want to be besieged with well-wishers wanting autographs and pics.

We order a couple of beers and some wings and settle onto opposite sides of the booth.

"What's going on?"

I rub at the tightness spreading across my chest as I prepare to voice my concerns for the first time. "I'm not sure being a house husband is for me."

Surprise splays across his face. "I thought you loved being home with the kids."

"I do, but I need more. I feel so fucking guilty saying that. Like I don't adore my kids and my husband. As if they aren't my entire world."

"No one who knows you would ever doubt your devotion to your family, Austen. You love them. Live for them. It's plain to see."

"So, why can't it be enough? Why do I feel so unfulfilled?"

"I think it's understandable. You had a busy career with a crazy schedule. You were traveling a lot. You went from that to a stay-at-home dad. Your life altered completely. You wouldn't be human if you weren't feeling unfulfilled. What about Tenley Ink though? I thought you were more involved in the business now."

"That was the plan, but it hasn't panned out like that. Keats is releasing new cookbooks every year, and the publishers have him traveling up and down the US doing publicity. When he's gone, I'm busy with the kids and the house. I oversee the accounts, and I've been working on our franchise plan, but I can't remember the last time I got to ink. Finding time to sketch is even challenging. Lia is super clingy and extremely shy. She is so attached to me, and it's hard to leave her. Alex is the only person besides Keats and me she's comfortable with."

"I'm no kid expert, as we both know"—he smirks —"but that seems like something you need to nip in the bud ASAP."

We stop talking when the waitress arrives with our beers. She tries to be discreet, but the blush creeping up her neck gives her away. Neither of us may be playing in the NFL anymore, but that doesn't mean we aren't noticed when we go out in public. Especially with both of us together. We were teammates in college and the first few years in the NFL.

She leaves without saying anything, and I give her major brownie points for letting us be.

"Have you told Keats this?" Colt asks, stretching one arm out over the back of the booth.

I shake my head. "He's been stressed lately, and I didn't want to add to it."

"You need to talk to him. Tell him how you're feeling so you can work something out between you. The solution is staring you in the face."

"I know." I knock back a mouthful of beer. "I want to be more hands-on at Tenley Ink, but the thought of hiring a nanny to take care of the kids doesn't sit well with me either."

"At least you have options. That's what I've been telling myself when I start throwing a pity party."

"And no money worries," I add. "I know I'm fortunate. It's why I've been feeling such horrendous guilt."

"Don't do that, dude. You are entitled to your feelings. It doesn't make you a bad father or husband if you want more for yourself. Some would argue it'd make you a better one."

"When the fuck did you get so wise?"

"I'm not sure I did, but I've been spending time with Carly and the kids, and it helps to put things into perspective."

Carly is Colton's big sister, and she was recently widowed. Her husband was in the army and killed overseas, leaving her with three kids under twelve. "How is she doing?"

"She's struggling." Worry lines furrow his brow. "At least I was able to alleviate her financial concerns and move her closer to my parents. When I see what she is dealing with, it makes my problems seem inconsequential."

"Have you made any plans?"

"Not a single one. I have no clue what I want to do with my life now. Football is all I've known."

"You have a business degree from Berkeley and resources to set up your own business. You could do something sports related. Become an agent or set up a sports facility. Those altitude training gyms are really taking off now, and that market is wide-open. You could open a franchise and go after the NFL business. Only a few teams use altitude training, like the Jets and the Falcons. You're ideally positioned to pitch the idea to them. Keats and I did a couple of sessions before we did our last big climb, and it was fucking brilliant. It's not just preparation for going to high altitudes or only for professional sports teams. It has been proven to help with weight loss, injury recovery, strength, and cardiovascular performance, so it has mass market appeal. Or you could always coach, if you don't want to go the business route?"

"You really think altitude training is a good opportunity?"

"I do. I might even be interested in getting involved if you decide to pursue it."

Colt sits up straighter and leans across the table. "I'm not sure I'd be brave enough to go it alone, but if you want in, then I'm definitely interested."

Excitement bubbles up my throat at the prospect of a new possibility. "Let me talk to Keats and sort out my family situation first, and then we can seriously discuss it."

Chapter Fourteen

Keaton

I'm exhausted as I turn the key in the lock of our front door, smothering a yawn as I drag my cases behind me and step into our large hall.

Home sweet home.

There is no greater feeling after two weeks away from my family.

A layer of stress instantly lifts from my shoulders as I softly close the door behind me. The familiar scent of jasmine and lavender tickles my nostrils as I dump my cases against the wall and remove my shoes. It's three a.m., and the house is deep in slumber.

"Hey," someone with a husky masculine voice says, and I almost jump out of my skin.

"Jesus, fuck, Austen. You scared the shit out of me!"

My husband smirks, pushing off the doorway to the living room and sauntering toward me. His thin pajama pants hang off toned hips, the material doing little to hide the sizable cock hanging between his muscular thighs.

"Welcome home," he says, and we fall into one another's arms.

"I've missed you so much. Missed home." I almost choke on the words, but it's no lie. I can't do this anymore. I hate these separations. It's killing me being away from my family.

"We missed you too," he says, tipping my head back and claiming my mouth in a hard kiss.

We stay wrapped around one another in the hallway, kissing and groping like we're horny teenagers. Every sweep of my husband's lips against mine, every stroke of his tongue, and every sensual caress helps to eradicate more of my tension until I'm a puddle of goo in his arms. His erection presses against the seam of my jeans where my cock is straining against the zipper.

"You must be tired," Austen says when we finally break apart. His fingers brush the skin underneath my eyes. "You look tired."

"I am," I truthfully reply, grabbing his ass and pulling him into me. "But not too tired to fuck my gorgeous husband."

"I didn't wait up for that," Austen says, gliding his hand in between our bodies. His skillful fingers trace the length of my cock through my jeans, and a bead of precum leaks from the tip. "I knew I wouldn't sleep until you were safely home."

"I love you," I say before pressing a tender kiss to his lips. "And I'm never too tired to fuck. I need you, babe."

"You have me. Always."

Austen takes my hand, leading me upstairs. I stop at the kids' bedrooms, opening the doors like a thief and stealing a peek at my handsome son and our beautiful little daughter. We used an anonymous donor egg, a surrogate, and IVF to deliver our first biological child. We both donated sperm and chose not to identify which of us fathered Lia, because it doesn't matter. We are both her fathers, irrespective of whose DNA she shares. But it's obvious she is Austen's biological child because she has his piercing green eyes and the same high cheekbones.

The second we close our bedroom door, I'm on my husband, pushing him back against the door and smashing my lips against his. My hand slides beneath his thin pajama pants, and I moan into his mouth when my fingers curl around his warm, hard, velvety-soft shaft.

Austen unbuttons my jeans, and his hand dives into my boxers. Our kissing grows heated, as we jerk one another off, until it feels like I'm about to explode. "I won't last. This is gonna be fast," I say, ripping my lips from his. I yank his pants down his legs, freeing his impressive cock.

"Top or bottom?" Austen asks, lifting a brow.

"Don't play games, baby. Hands on door, ass out."

He smirks as he withdraws his hand from my boxers, pulling them and my jeans down my legs as I whip my shirt up over my head. Austen crouches naked in front of me, removing my sneakers and helping me to get rid of my jeans and underwear. Then he kneels between my thighs and takes my erection into his mouth. My palms flatten against the door as I lean over while my husband sucks me off.

"Fuck, stop." I tug on his dark hair after a few minutes. "I want to come in your ass."

Austen rises to his full height, grabbing my face and kissing me hard. "I know what you need." He walks to the bedside table, grabbing the lube from the drawer. I watch his stately stride as he returns to me, admiring the hard planes and toned curves of his muscular body. Although he's not subjected to rigorous training sessions anymore, he works out a lot in our home gym, and we regularly take the kids hiking, kayaking, swimming, and mountain biking. My husband is fit as fuck and hot as fuck, and I can't wait to nail that tight ass.

"You're drooling, famous one," he teases, brushing his thumb against the corner of my mouth.

"Shut up and get into position."

"Bossy." Austen nips at my lower lip. "I love it and you."

I kiss him hard before pushing him toward the door. Flattening his palms against it, he tips his ass up and spreads his legs. I walk behind him while applying lube to my dick, which is already wet from Austen's lush mouth. Lubing a few fingers, I insert them slowly and carefully into my husband's ass, gently pushing past that soft ridge of resistance until I'm all the way through. I warm him up in measured strokes, probing the tight walls of his rectum as I slide my fingers in and out until he's ready for me.

Then I inch inside him, until I'm fully in, and fuck him hard. I swat his hand away from his dick, and I take over, stroking him in sync with the thrusts of my cock in his ass, and it doesn't take long to reach a peak. Ripples of pleasure course through me, and we descend into bliss together as we both come at the same time. Cum sprays the back of the door and drips from my fingers onto the hardwood floor while I fill my husband's ass with my seed.

I drape myself over him, holding him tight as I savor the moment, loving how comforting and solid he feels underneath me. Austen has always had a way of grounding me, and now is no different. Pressing a line of kisses down his spine, I whisper, "I love you."

"I love you too." Austen straightens up as I pull out of his ass, licking my lips while I watch my cum leak down the backs of his thighs. Damn. Is there anything hotter?

"Shower with me?" I ask, lacing my sticky fingers in his.

He nods, and we walk to our en suite bathroom together, sated and content. We take a quick shower and dry off, clean up the mess at the door, and then crawl under the covers of our king-sized bed. Lying on our sides, we face one another with our bodies pressed close together. We kiss for a bit before tiredness overwhelms me, and I practically yawn into his mouth. "Sleep, babe." Austen urges my head to his chest, and I go willingly, resting my cheek against his toned pecs.

"Can we go camping tomorrow?" I ask. "Take the RV up to Wompatuck and just spend some time together as a family?" I need to talk to Austen, and I'd like to do it while we are relaxing, surrounded by nature. Wompatuck State Park is near Hingham, which is only a forty-five-minute drive from here. They have tons of campgrounds with electrical utilities for RV campers and plenty of trails for hiking and mountain biking. I desperately need to escape the stress and hustle and bustle of the last few weeks, and I always feel chilled out when camping.

"I'd like that, and you know the kids will be over the moon."

"Good." I struggle to keep my eyes open as my arms wrap around my husband's back. "Let's leave after breakfast."

"Daddy, you're home!" Eliot races across the kitchen floor and throws himself at me. "Did Dad tell you I came first in the swim competition yesterday?"

"He did." I lie purely because there wasn't time for Austen to tell me yet, but I know he would have if he wasn't busy packing up the RV while I make breakfast. "Well done. I'm proud of you." I lift my son into my arms and hold him in a bear hug. This is what life is all about, and I'm sick of missing out on memories I can't ever reclaim.

"Daddy!" Lia shrieks when she sees me, running toward me at speed. She only turned three recently, and she's still got cute chubby legs and arms, but she's already losing her baby face. I set Eliot on his feet and crouch down, opening my arms for my daughter. She flies at me, climbing me like a tree, pressing her face into my neck and hugging me tight. "Me missed you," she says over a sob. "Don't go."

My heart is breaking as I hold her tight and close my eyes. "Daddy's home now, and he's not going anywhere," I say, opening my eyes and rising with Lia in my arms.

Austen stands in the doorway, a pained expression on his face. "Breakfast is ready," I tell him, walking toward the table. I glance around, looking for Lia's high chair, but it appears to be missing. I glance over my shoulder at my husband. "Where's Lia's chair?"

Lia lifts her head, pinning me with a proud, goofy smile. "Me a big girl now." She wriggles to get down, and I let her.

"We wanted to surprise you," Austen says, helping Lia up onto one of the chairs around our long rectangular kitchen table. There is a plastic booster seat strapped to the base of the chair.

"Wow. You are a real big girl now." My heart swells with pride as I watch Austen buckle the straps around her waist and gently push her in closer to the table.

"Are we going camping?" Eliot asks, grabbing some crispy bacon, fried potatoes, and eggs from the center of the table. "I saw the RV out front."

"Yes." Austen narrows his eyes at our son. "Use your fork, not your fingers."

Eliot rolls his eyes, ignoring Austen as he stuffs scrambled eggs into his mouth with his fingers.

"We only bring good well-behaved children camping with us, so unless you want us to drop you at Nanny and Grandad's, I suggest you pick up your fork and do what your dad says," I tell him. We made a rule before the kids came into our lives that we would always be on the same page in front of them, and we never disagree when they are in earshot either.

Eliot picks up his fork without further protest, like I knew he would. Eliot loves the outdoors, which isn't much of a surprise as we've been taking him hiking since he was a toddler.

"Everyone, eat," Austen says, taking a seat beside Lia. "And then we'll be on our way."

"They are both asleep," I say, stepping outside the RV later that night, carrying a couple of blankets. It can get a little chilly at this altitude at this time of night.

"I'm not surprised. We wore them out today."

I chuckle as I toss a blanket at my husband and drop into the portable lounge chair beside him. "That we did." I drape the blanket over my legs as Austen hands me a cold beer from the ice chest.

"I'm glad we came up here today," he says, as I rest my head on his shoulder. "Being at one with nature always puts problems into perspective."

"We're in an RV. I'd hardly call it being one with nature," I tease. "But I know what you mean." We found a spot to camp that is completely isolated, and it has stunning views. The only sounds are the clicking noises of cicadas and crickets and the soft rustling of leaves from the surrounding trees.

Raising my head, I take Austen's hand in my free one as I lift my beer to my lips. It's only then his words properly register. "What problems?"

Austen squeezes my hand as he turns to face me. "I wanted to talk to you about something."

"Me too."

"You go first."

"I want to put my career on ice for a while." I just put it out there because there is no easing into it. The shock on Austen's face isn't a surprise. I haven't given him any indication I'm unhappy because I didn't want to seem ungrateful. He was devastated when injury meant he had to quit the Patriots two years ago. It seems thoughtless to be purposely putting my dream on hold when his was forcibly taken from him.

"Is it the traveling?"

I nod. "Mostly, but I could keep doing *The Queer Kitchen Revolution*. That isn't as taxing, and at least I can do it from home, but it's more than that." I set my beer down on the rugged ground beside my chair. "I want to spend time with the kids without the pressures of work, and I want us to try for another baby. I'd like to have a bio kid of my own. Not that it really matters, because I love Eliot and Lia equally, but I love seeing parts of you in our daughter, and I want that for you."

"I want that too," he readily admits, "but I can't reconcile that need with the restlessness I've been feeling."

My eyes probe his. "What don't I know?"

"I didn't want to say anything when you were already so stressed, but I need to go back to work. I love the kids, and I love that I get to spend so much time with them, but—"

"You need more," I finish for him.

"It's selfish, I know."

"Babe, no." I clasp his face in my hands. "It is not selfish to want something else in your life. This isn't a surprise, and I have suspected as much. I was waiting for you to broach this subject. You have worked hard your entire life, and I know you want to be more involved in Tenley Ink. You need to chase your passion, and I would never stop you from pursuing it." My hands lower to his lap.

"Are you saying what you're saying because of this? The last thing I want is you giving up your career for mine. We have other options. We can hire a nanny."

"Nope." I shake my head. "I know we could, but I want to be with them. I'm saying this because of where my head is at. Plus, I'm not giving up my career. I'm just taking some time off. We are fortunate we can do this. When I feel like returning to work, we can look into a part-time nanny, or maybe I won't ever feel like going back." I shrug. "I don't know, but I didn't set up my own business to be stressed and so freaking lonely without my family. That's not living to me."

Austen smiles wide as he presses his brow to mine. "We are always so much in tandem with one another." He eases back so he can look me in the eye. "I was feeling so selfish and guilty, thinking how we'd have to hire a nanny, but this is perfect."

"It is." I kiss his lips softly. "You go do your thing, and let me be the house husband. Nothing would make me happier."

An amorous grin crosses his delectable mouth as he

leans in, pressing his warm lips to my ear. "I think my dick in your ass might be the cherry on top."

"Is that a promise?" I say, my tone lowering a level as blood rushes south.

"Damn straight." He stands, tugging me up with him, and our arms wrap around one another. "Think you can be quiet?"

I brush strands of dark hair back off his brow. "For you, I can be anything you need me to be."

"I only ever want you to be yourself, Keats." Tears glisten in his eyes. "Because you are so fucking perfect, and I will love you until my dying breath."

Chapter Fifteen
Keven

I step into the glass elevator of the prestigious building in Boston and press the button for the top floor. Turning around, I admire the view of the harbor as I shoot toward the office space occupied by S.I.S.S., which is an acronym for Superhero IT Support Services. My lips curve of their own volition, and without knowing it, I can guess Xavier Daniels is behind the quirky name. Somehow, I don't see the straitlaced Sawyer Hunt suggesting it. Though, he did don a superhero costume, complete with a cape, and hang a large banner of the image along the side of his father's old office building in New York when he was trying to win his man back.

It must have worked because they have been happily married for years, and the IT consultancy business they co-own maintains a high reputation within the industry and with high-profile clients.

Which is why I am here to meet with them. They have asked me several times, in the past few years, if I would come work with them, but the timing was never right.

Until now.

The elevator opens into a narrow, carpeted hallway, and I head toward the set of wooden double doors in front of me. I press the button on the wall-mounted keypad, announcing myself to the woman who replies. Then I'm buzzed into the plush reception area, where one-half of the brains behind this operation is waiting for me.

"It's okay, Delilah," Xavier says, glancing over his shoulder at the pretty young receptionist with the sparkly purple-framed glasses. "Keven doesn't need to sign in. I'll take it from here."

"No problem, Xavier," Delilah says, sending me a flirty smile as she gives me a quick once-over.

Xavier strides toward me, wearing a big grin and a bright red skinny-fit suit with a black shirt. His famous faux hawk is back, and he has it dyed pink, in a look similar to the one MGK is sporting these days. A myriad of tattoos and piercings adorn his tall, toned, lean frame. He looks more like a rock star than a tech genius, and he's one of the most entertaining, interesting people I know. "Welcome. It's good to see you, man," he says.

"You too. Thanks for agreeing to meet with me."

He slaps me on the back, and I'm conscious of eyes watching our every move.

"Ignore her," Xavier whispers, jerking his head and motioning for me to walk with him. "She's the biggest flirt." I slant him an amused grin because everyone knows there is no bigger flirt than the man walking beside me.

Xavier chuckles. "Okay, maybe not the biggest. I can't go handing my crown to anyone, you know, but it's all in good fun. She's a great receptionist. Discreet and efficient and worth her weight in gold."

He presses his thumb to the keypad beside a set of frosted glass double doors, and they slide open a few seconds later. "I thought I'd give you a quick tour before we meet Grumpy."

I lift a brow. "Grumpy?"

Xavier stops just inside the door of the large open-plan floor space. "My husband has been a moody prick all week, but I'm sure he'll be polite to you. No one explains how success goes hand in hand with stress. I'm able to leave a large portion of that at the door when we leave every night, but Sawyer carries it with him like an invisible load on his back. Which is one of the reasons we were delighted to get your call." He eyeballs me, shielding nothing. "I'm not going to beat around the bush. Hunt will probably bust my balls for laying it on the line, but he can take his aggression out on my ass later."

I snort out a laugh, grinning widely. There is no denying working closely with Xavier and Sawyer will be far more entertaining than my current job at the bureau.

"We need you," Xavier continues, his expression and tone serious. "You can name your price if our proposal isn't to your liking."

"Proposal?"

"I'll let Hunt explain," Xavier says, lifting a shoulder and urging me to walk.

"It's not about the money," I say, falling into line

beside him. "For me, it's about job satisfaction and finding a role that will better suit my family life."

"We are very flexible," Xavier explains as we walk past row upon row of workstations. "Our HR person is the bomb, and she has implemented cutting-edge policies and programs that have seen our retention rate rise."

Most everyone wears headphones or earbuds, and they are bent over expensive laptops and desktop computers, tapping away on keyboards. A few people congregate in groups, heads bent together, deep in discussion. There is no formal dress code, and the men and women I see before me are wearing a vast array of clothing. Brightly colored framed prints adorn the walls, and there are potted plants and flowers dotted all over the place. Desks overflow with personal paraphernalia. In all corners of the room, there are small coffee stations with adjacent water dispensers.

"The people you see here make up only a fraction of our workforce. Many of our teams work from their homes. We have employees all over the US and in different parts of the world. Because of the nature of our work, most of it can be done at times that suit the employees. We are deadline driven, and as long as the work is delivered on time, we don't care if they work one day out of seven, or work through the night, or duck out during the day to pick up their kids from school."

"That's commendable, but how do you ensure confidentiality and prevent data breaches?"

"We only recruit the best skilled and most trustworthy people. Everyone is thoroughly screened to ensure there are no skeletons in their closet. Rogan

Anderson is head of IT security, and he has built a robust system that alerts us if anyone tries to copy or print information or tries to log on from a different browser. We have processes in place that safeguard our information and the work we do. Thousands of our clients have deployed these systems, and it's a big selling point when we tell them we use these systems and processes ourselves."

Passion exudes from his tone and underscores every word, and he sounds the way I used to sound before the FBI sucked all the enjoyment from my work.

"This is the recreational room," Xavier says, opening a door to an expansive room with casual seating, a pool table, a large gaming area, and a few TVs. A jukebox and variety of candy machines line one wall. "Next door is the gym."

I trail him to the next space, poking my head into the well-equipped training area.

"The canteen is on the other side of the main working area. We provide free meals delivered by an in-house catering company who provides meal options to suit a wide variety of diets. We also hold regular after-hours events, like yoga, mindfulness, meditation, and we provide a subsidy to off-site staff so they can avail of similar services in their locality."

"Impressive." They have made themselves competitive with Silicon Valley, and that's no easy feat.

"A healthy body and mind equal a more productive employee. It's a no-brainer," he says, opening the door to a large conference room.

"This is our main meeting area, and the rest of the

doors you see on this side are smaller meeting rooms and breakout areas where the team can congregate to brainstorm."

We walk back the way we came, passing by the doors we entered, and I see three small offices tucked into the alcove with the reception area behind the wall at the rear and the main working area laid out before them. The offices are constructed completely of glass with blinds for privacy if needed. Xavier guides me into the last room, not even knocking before he swings the door open.

Sawyer Hunt is sitting behind the only desk in the room, and he raises his finger to his mouth, cautioning us to be quiet, as someone speaks through the large computer screen facing him.

"I'll have to call you back, Haruto," Sawyer says. "In the meantime, email me your list of questions." He ends the call and stands, smiling at me as he walks out from behind the glossy white desk. Xavier closes the door behind us. "Would it kill you to knock?" Sawyer says, narrowing his eyes at his husband.

"You've been saying that to me for years," Xavier replies with a grin. "It hasn't worked yet, and it never will."

Sawyer rolls his eyes as he strides toward me. "I've tried to knock some manners into him, but I might as well bang my head against a brick wall."

"Shut it, drill se—"

Sawyer glares at Xavier, cutting him off mid-speech. Xavier chuckles. "Works like a charm every time."

These two are known for butting heads, and I'm sure it keeps things interesting in their relationship. It wouldn't be for me. I like an easier life and I love how seamlessly Cheryl and I fit together. We get each other in a way most couples don't. I know I'm lucky. I definitely hit the jackpot with my wife.

"Ignore him," Sawyer says. "He loves winding me up, but he's far less irritating with everyone else." He extends his hand, and I shake it. "Thanks for dropping by. We were thrilled to get your call. Your timing couldn't be more perfect." He gestures toward the empty chairs in front of the desk. "Please take a seat."

I claim one of the chairs while Xavier claims the other, and Sawyer returns behind the desk. "Thank you for seeing me. I'm grateful for your time," I say.

"I'm not going to mince my words," Sawyer replies, proving he's as much of a straight shooter as his husband. "We want you to come work with us. This isn't news to you. Working with you as the FBI liaison on the few projects we have completed together has only cemented our view that you would be an asset to our company."

"Those projects are one of the reasons I'm sitting here today. Your professionalism and expertise are above reproach. I enjoyed working closely with both of you immensely. Your obvious passion is an added bonus. My role in the FBI has changed a lot over the years, taking me further and further away from IT, and I'm no longer happy."

"Not to mention how dangerous it is," Xavier says, pinning me with a knowing look. It's no secret I was shot on the job last year as it was widely reported in the media. They found out I was working with the bureau a year after I became a field agent, and the media intrusion is another reason I'm eager to get out now.

"What we do doesn't come without danger either," Sawyer warns. "The main face of our operation is the support services we offer to medium and large corporations, but you are aware we have a secret division that provides more specialist services."

"I am aware of the risk and prepared to accept it. Let's not pretend I haven't pulled tons of shady and illegal shit in my past. My skill set is perfectly aligned." S.I.S.S takes on top confidential consultancy projects for government and private clients, both individuals and firms, which amounts to spying, hacking, and other activities that would be considered illegal if it became public knowledge. A lot of parties have vested interests in keeping those activities on the down low, and with the structures and processes in place, it's unlikely it would ever get out in the public domain. If it did, S.I.S.S. could gain a lot of dangerous enemies, and we all could become targets.

"You don't need to sell yourself to us, Keven. We know what you can do. The only discussion is if you are in and in what capacity."

"I'm in," I say without hesitation. "I'm prepared to immediately resign from the FBI if I have your word there is a role for me here."

Sawyer slides an envelope across the table to me. "We took the liberty of preparing these in advance. Inside that envelope are two offers. We propose you go home, review them carefully, talk to your wife and your lawyer, and mull it over. Return on Monday morning, and we can talk it all through. Unless you need further time, then you can sign the relevant paperwork, and we can make it official."

"We are offering you two choices," Xavier says, elaborating. "To come on board as an employee in a senior management position with a seat on the board or invest in the business and become a joint owner with us."

My eyes pop wide, and I almost fall off my chair. "You are offering me the opportunity to buy into the business?"

They nod at the same time.

"Why? You can't need the money."

"We don't. What we need is a third opinion when it comes to making key decisions," Sawyer explains, drumming his fingers on the table. "Things can get heated when we disagree, and we think adding a third owner would help to make the decision-making process easier."

"It will also help to spread the workload and ease the pressure," Xavier adds.

"To be fully transparent, having you as co-owner of S.I.S.S. will add enormous benefit to our value proposition. You are a recognizable figure. Our clients will know you worked for the FBI, and that adds a legitimacy government clients will like."

"We're not being altruistic in offering this to you," Xavier says. "It will add a lot of value to our business and our lives, as it would yours. You mentioned outside you want to have more time for your family, and working with us will give you that."

"You can work your own hours, fitting it around your family requirements. You can also split your time between the office and home, but we insist at least one of us is here at all times. You need to be physically present here at least one day a week to be visible and available to staff members," Sawyer adds.

"That sounds very workable. I'm blown away, and I don't know what to say." I am genuinely shocked they appear to want me this much. Pleasantly so.

"Say yes." Xavier grins.

"I'll review this tonight and over the weekend, and I'll talk to Cheryl and my brother Kent. He's my lawyer."

"It might be prudent to bring him with you on Monday. I can have our legal counsel here too," Sawyer says. "That way, if you have any legal questions or request any amendments to the contract, it will expedite the matter."

"Sounds good. I'll call Kent on my way home and see if he's available."

"Excellent." Sawyer stands, walking around the desk again, and I rise, holding the envelope in my hand. "We would love to welcome you into our company as a co-owner, but if you decide the employee route is best for you at this time, we shall accept that. We can always revisit the other option at a later time."

Xavier gets up too. "What Hunt means is we will take you any way we can get you, Keven."

Sawyer mutters under his breath and glares at his husband. "We'll just pretend he didn't say that." We shake hands again. "You have our numbers. If you need to ask us anything between now and Monday, call anytime."

"Thank you both. I can't even describe how much it means that you would trust me like this."

"You're a good person, Keven. The kind of guy we want in our corner," Xavier says.

"Your family has been good to us and our friends over the years as you have too. This feels like the most natural fit to us," Sawyer supplies.

"It really does," I agree. "And the timing is right in a way it wasn't before."

"I love it when a plan comes together," Xavier says, rubbing his hands in glee, and I chuckle. He's like an excitable kid at the best of times. That, combined with his eclectic sense of dress, and it's easy to forget he's one of the world's biggest tech geniuses.

"We look forward to hearing your decision on Monday," Sawyer says. "Xavier will walk you out."

Chapter Sixteen
Cheryl

I hear a car pull up in front of our house, and I turn around in the kitchen, looking out the large front window to see who it is. Only family has the security code to the gate, but I'm not expecting any visitors. My eyes pop wide when I spot my husband getting out of his X5 with a massive bouquet of flowers and a bottle of champagne. A thrill shoots through me comingled with alarm when I notice the time on my cell. Keven is never home from work this early, and I instantly worry something has happened.

Wiping my hands down the front of my apron, I untie it, dump it on the counter, and walk out of the kitchen into the hallway. The front door opens, and my gorgeous husband steps into our house. Kev deposits his laptop bag on the hall table as he flashes me a winning smile, and my heart soars behind my chest cavity. A small skinny form whizzes by my legs, racing toward the door. "Daddy's home!" Talisa yells, to alert her brother, before she barrels into Kev, wrapping herself around his legs. Our five-year-old is the biggest daddy's girl. She adores Keven, and I love the close bond they have.

"What's wrong?" Taylor asks, coming up alongside me. "Why are you home this early?"

Pain stretches across Keven's face as our son's words dig deep. He messes the top of Talisa's long blonde hair, walking toward us with her holding on to his leg, being lifted on his foot. "Nothing is wrong, son," he says, leaning in to kiss me as he hands me the flowers. "Everything is great." He rubs his thumb across our son's puckered brow. "Don't worry so much."

"You got shot, Dad. I can't stop worrying."

Taylor's words pierce my chest, and I know Keven hates the anxiety our seven-year-old son suffers from now because he was shot on the job last year. Taylor has had nightmares and panic attacks as his fear of losing his father reaches deep into his subconscious. It has gotten a little better these past few months, but how can I tell my kid to stop worrying his father will get killed when it's my greatest fear too? Which is why... "Oh, you had that meeting today. That's why you're back early." Today was a manic day, and in all my rushing around, I forgot. "How did it go?"

"Amazing." Keven beams at me as he lifts Talisa on to his back. "A celebration is in order," he adds, waving the bottle of expensive champagne in front of me.

I immediately feel several layers of stress leave my strung-out body. "I want to hear all about it. You can fill me in while I finish making dinner." I turn my attention to our children. "Is your homework finished?"

"Homework is stupid," Talisa says the same time Taylor shakes his head.

"Homework is important," Keven says, setting our daughter back on her feet. "Both of you finish your homework while I talk to Mommy. If you do a good job, I'll take you out for ice cream after dinner."

I have never seen two kids more eager to return to their homework as our spawn races around the corner and back to the study I share with them. Keven has his own home office, because his work is super confidential, and the kids aren't allowed in there. I do most of my work from the studio I own in downtown Boston, but I have a dark room here where I develop and hang some of my photos, and I do the administration and accounts work from my desk in the study.

"Thank you for these," I say, nuzzling my nose in the flowers as Keven slings his arm around my shoulders and we walk into the kitchen. "They're gorgeous."

"Not as gorgeous as you." I turn my head, and we share another quick kiss.

"If you're planning to get laid tonight, you are doing and saying all the right things."

"Celebration sex is my favorite," he murmurs, sliding his hand down the side of my body to squeeze my ass.

"I thought makeup sex was your favorite," I tease, taking the flowers to the sink as Keven opens one of the overhead cupboards, removing a large glass vase and handing it to me.

"I love makeup sex too," he says, pressing his body against my back and sweeping my hair aside, as I fill the vase with water. "But I hate it has to come after an argument because I hate arguing with you. Hence why celebration sex trumps makeup sex." He plants a slew of soft kisses up and down the side of my neck.

"I hate arguing too," I admit as I position the flowers in the vase. Setting it on the counter beside the sink, I turn around in my husband's arms. "I know we have been arguing a lot lately, but it's only because I am so worried." Keven was seriously injured last year, and I will never forget getting that call. I had heart palpitations the entire car journey to the hospital, and I burst into floods of tears when I saw my husband lying unconscious on the bed, hooked up to numerous machines. "Seeing you in the hospital scared the absolute shit out of me, Keven. I love that you do so much good through your work, but I hate the danger and the risks to your safety." I sweep my hands through his dark hair. "I don't want anything to happen to you. You know this." We have discussed this time and time again.

"Which is one of the reasons why I called Sawyer and Xavier. I know you wanted me to quit immediately after the shooting, but I couldn't leave my team in the lurch in the middle of a case. I needed to see it through to completion, and now I have, I can put the bureau behind me."

"It went well then?"

"Well enough that I will be resigning on Monday morning even though I haven't even looked at the offers Sawyer and Xavier have written up for me."

Tears prick my eyes as I fling my arms around him. "I am so relieved, honey. I would die if anything happened to you."

His strong arms band around me, and he holds me close. "As I would if anything happened to you or the kids. If I believed there was a real risk to me or my family after the shooting, I would have quit immediately, but the threat had been neutralized at the scene." He tilts my head back, clasping my face in his large palms. "I never wanted to upset or disappoint you, but I wanted to walk away with a pristine record and my reputation intact. I hate how much you have worried about me, and I hate what it's done to Taylor. Hopefully, me leaving the FBI will reassure him, and his nightmares and panic attacks will stop."

"Dr. Fleming seems to believe it will help enormously, but she advised we continue bringing him to therapy."

"Whatever he needs." Kev hugs me again, dotting kisses into my hair.

We enjoy a family meal together before Kev takes the kids to the local ice cream parlor while I finish up some work. Switching off the light in the study a couple of hours later, I step into the hallway as Kev emerges from upstairs.

"All good?" I ask, walking to meet him.

"They are both asleep."

I snuggle into his side, and we walk together toward the living room, where the champagne is already on ice.

"I talked with Taylor. I told him I'm leaving the FBI, and he seemed relieved."

"I know I am," I admit as I sink into the couch.

Kev pours two glasses of champagne, and we settle beside one another, reviewing the paperwork Sawyer and Xavier gave him and discussing the pros and cons of both offers. "What do you think I should do?" Kev asks after we have put the paperwork aside and poured fresh glasses of champagne.

"I think you should do whatever makes you the happiest and whatever makes the most sense for you. This isn't about money. It's about job satisfaction and your personal and professional needs."

"I think I'd be happy with either option, but being part owner gives me a greater say in the direction the company takes and the type of clients we take on. A large part of my frustration in the FBI these past few years has been the lack of control. It's frustrating having to do something you wholeheartedly disagree with, knowing it's the wrong decision."

"Then sign on as a co-owner."

"It's a big investment. More than we have."

"S.I.S.S. is a very successful, growing business, and its market value reflects that. Buying in won't be cheap, but it's a good investment with great return potential. You could ask your parents for a loan, go to the bank for a loan, or take them up on their offer of paying a lump sum now and then the rest on a monthly basis from your salary. They are making it as easy as possible for you to co-own the business, and I think that speaks volumes."

Kev nods, looking thoughtful. "I definitely got that vibe. Three's not a crowd when it comes to business."

"Talk to your mom or Kade and Eva. Hell, you could talk to any number of people within the family. Kyler knows finance. Kent can cover the legal aspect. Selena and Keanu, Presley, Austen, and Keats all run successful businesses. See what everyone thinks, and then mull it all over."

"I will because I don't want to take unnecessary risks with our finances or our future even if my gut is telling me the co-owner route is the right option."

"You know I'll back you whatever you decide. I trust your judgment, and I want you to be happy."

"I already feel so much happier, and I haven't even resigned or signed on the dotted line. This just feels right."

"I'm glad, honey." I sip my champagne as I snuggle into his side. "I have some news of my own."

He looks down at me. "You found a manager?"

I nod. "I did. At long last." I have been trying to hire someone to manage my studio because it's all become too much for me and I'm working crazy hours. It's been hectic trying to juggle work and family life, and I needed to make changes. I hired a new photographer three months ago, and she's working out great, but I couldn't find the right person to help me to manage the business. I was despairing of hiring anyone. "I should've asked Faye to handle the recruitment from the outset," I admit, running my fingers back and forth across Kev's leg through his pants. "She had a shortlist of suitably quali-fied people for me within two weeks. She personally headhunted them, so they fit my requirements. In the end, I could have had my pick."

"When does your new hire start?"

"John has to work two weeks' notice at his current job, but he'll start after that. I will need to train him, but I reckon two months from now I can officially cut my hours and be home more."

"I have great flexibility with my new job too," Kev says, taking my almost empty flute and putting it down on the coffee table alongside his. His eyes sparkle with happiness. "You know what this means?"

I crawl into his lap and straddle his thighs. "We can prioritize getting pregnant again." We are both aching for more kids, and we don't want to leave it any longer because our kids are getting older and we're not getting any younger. We have had to put it off because we knew, practically, that we couldn't expand our family until we reworked our job situation. Now that we have, there is nothing holding us back.

"Want to start working on that now?" my sexy husband says, sliding his hands underneath my dress and palming the bare cheeks of my ass.

"Do you even have to ask?" I pin him with a sultry grin as I pop the button on his pants and drag the zipper down. "We have more reasons to celebrate now, and I can't wait to expand our family."

Those are the last words spoken for a very long time.

Chapter Seventeen

Alex

"We'd better get showered and dressed before everyone arrives and we gross them out," I say, giggling as I peel myself off my husband's sweat-slickened chest.

"Remind me again why we thought it was a good idea to invite all the kids and grandkids when we could've stayed in bed all weekend making love?" James asks, his eyes darkening with renewed lust as I slide off his naked body and push to my feet.

"Because our family is finally properly reunited, and that is a cause to celebrate." I lean down and kiss him. "Besides, the kids return to school next week, and it's our last opportunity for a summer party. We still have tomorrow to fornicate to our hearts' desire."

James barks out a laugh, playfully swatting my ass. "Fornicate? I think you're showing your age, darling," he teases.

"Don't remind me," I murmur, heading toward the door that leads to our en suite bathroom.

"Hey." The bed squeaks as James climbs out. His arms encircle my waist from behind. "You are still every bit as beautiful as the day I met you. I can't believe you will be sixty next year. You don't look a day over twenty."

Now it's my turn to laugh. I angle my head and look back at my husband smiling. "You are so full of shit, but I love you."

"I love you too." He bends down and kisses my lips, and I melt against him. I never thought we would have this again. I thought James was lost to me forever, and I had made my peace, of sorts, with it.

In hindsight, separating was the best thing to happen to us. It allowed us time to heal from the pain we had caused one another, develop a deep friendship and coparent relationship, learn to enjoy each other's company, and rediscover our love. It helped to put things into perspective. To realize what we had and stood to lose if we divorced. Now, things are better than ever between us, and we have the type of relationship I have always craved.

"You know what?" I swivel in my husband's arms. "I am going to embrace turning sixty. I don't believe I have ever been happier or more content than I am now." I slide my hands up his impressive chest. My husband takes pride in his appearance, and he still looks hot for his age. He plays golf regularly, works out every day in the gym, and we go for an early morning jog together each day, weather permitting. He is lean and toned, with a body men half his age would kill for. The thick gray streaks in his dark hair make him look distinguished, and I am as attracted to him as I was when I first set eyes on him.

"We are rock solid. Our kids and grandkids are all happy and healthy. We got to retire early, and we have the money to travel and do whatever we want. We are so fortunate, and life doesn't get much better than this."

"Doesn't it?" James scoops me up and throws me over his shoulder as I shriek. "Because I have it on good authority that shower sex is the bomb."

JAMES

"It's a great day for a barbecue," Kade says, coming up to the grill.

"That it is," I agree, squinting through my sunglasses as I look up at the radiant sun casting rays of warm golden sunshine on the ground below.

Laughter rings out behind me, and I turn around, smiling as I watch all my grandkids splashing about in the pool. Thankfully, we have a new Olympic-sized outdoor pool to house the myriad of colorful floats and plastic balls and toys the little ones come with. Their parents and my stunning wife are draped across loungers around the pool, sipping cocktails that Presley, Cheryl, Rachel, and Faye made.

Selena is the only adult drinking a mocktail. It warms my heart to see the growing bump on her stomach. Keanu and his wife tried for a long time to have children, and it's wonderful it's coming true for them now. Their adopted son Jett is moving in with them on Monday. They tried to speed it up so he could be here today, but it wasn't possible.

It's probably for the best. We're not exactly quiet when we are all together. It's a lot to take in. We would most likely have scared the troubled teen. I know Alex will organize another family dinner in a few weeks after he has settled into his new home, and he can meet everyone then.

Kal and Kent are setting up freestanding speakers and hooking it up to some contraption that holds their iPhones and plays music. I can't keep up with the technology available today. Not that I need to when I have a computer genius son in Keven. We are so relieved he has quit the FBI. It was becoming far too dangerous, and he has more than paid them back for his teenage misdemeanors.

"Are you going to just stand there or help?" Kyler says, arching a brow at his older brother.

"Haven't you heard that saying about too many cooks?" Kade gestures between me, Kyler, and Brad. With so many mouths to feed on a regular basis, Alex had three industrial-sized grills built the same time she got the new pool installed. We have a fully equipped outdoor kitchen along with an expansive new patio area. Four new large wooden circular tables and chairs accommodate the entire family. "I think I'll leave you to it."

"Lazy shit," Kyler murmurs under his breath as Kade slinks away.

"Don't let your mother hear you saying that. She's on a high today, and no one or nothing is going to put a dampener on her joy."

"Relax, Dad. I was only joking. Sorta," he adds, sharing a grin with Brad. Brad and Rachel are living with Faye and Kyler right now while they house hunt for their own place in Wellesley. I know my niece-slash-daughter-in-law is thrilled to have her best friend back on US soil, and Brad and Ky are thick as thieves again.

An hour later, we are all seated at tables, and the scent of chargrilled meat wafts in the air, rumbling tummies.

"I want to make a toast," Alex says before the vultures demolish the mountainous plates of food.

"Hang on," Eva says, standing. "We need champagne for this." Austen and Presley join Eva in pouring champagne and offering flutes around. Hewson and Milly distribute mocktails to the kids and a fresh one to Selena. When everyone has a drink, we raise our glasses high as my wife makes her toast. "To the Kennedys. To family. To always supporting and loving one another through all the ups and downs. To success and happiness. To living our dreams."

"Hear, hear." A chorus of agreement rings out as heads bob, glasses chink, and drinks are drunk.

I stand and round the table, wrapping an arm around my wife's shoulders. "We love you all very much, and we're so proud of you. Family is the greatest enjoyment life has to offer, and every one of you enhances our lives in so many ways. Thank you for being here with us today. You mean the world to your mom and me."

HEWSON

I pace the garden at the side of my grandparents' house, out of sight of the oldies, who are partying like they are born-again teenagers and they won't wake up with pounding headaches, sick stomachs, and excitable kids jumping all over them.

Nausea swims up my throat as the words lodge in my brain, and I almost throw up as reality knocks on my skull. "I am so fucked, so fucked, so fucked," I murmur to myself, doing a damn good impression of a complete nutjob.

"Why are you so fucked?" a man with a deep familiar voice asks from the shadows underneath the side of the house. Kyler steps forward, his tall, broad, muscular form highlighted under the glow of the moon.

"Jesus. You almost gave me a coronary." Panic bubbles up my throat as I contemplate how to avoid answering my uncle. I narrow my eyes as he draws closer. "Is that a joint?"

A smirk toys with his lips. "It is, but don't tell. Your grandma would throw a hissy fit."

"Pass it over and I won't."

"Not a chance," Kyler says, taking a long drag on the joint and blowing smoke circles into the air. "Your mother would string me up if she knew I gave you weed."

It's not as if I haven't smoked MJ before, but I don't admit that out loud, for obvious reasons.

"Don't think I haven't noticed how you ignored my question," my godfather says, eyeing me with concern on his face.

"It doesn't matter." I shrug as if my life hasn't just upended.

"Hewson." Kyler stubs the joint out between his fingers, rolling it up carefully and tucking it in the back pocket of his shorts. "If you are in trouble, you can talk to me."

"You'll tell my parents."

He moves in front of me and tips his head up a little. I'm taller than my dad and all my uncles now, with the exception of Kaden who still has an inch on me. If I keep growing, I'll outgrow him too. "Is this something they need to know?"

Hell no. Yes. Maybe. I don't know. I shrug.

"You're worrying me," he adds.

"I'm not your kid. You don't need to worry about me."

"You're my nephew and my godson. Asking me not to worry about you, or any of my nieces and nephews, is as futile as Kanye West spouting his desire to be the leader of the world." He clamps his hand on my shoulder. "If you need help, let me help you. Tell me what's going on."

I shuck out of his hold and start pacing again. I want to tell him, but I'm scared. "I don't know what to do," I admit, lifting my head as I prowl back and forth on the manicured lawn. "I have fucked up so bad. Mom is going to be devastated. Dad will kick my ass for being so fucking stupid. You'll think I'm an idiot. All my uncles will. Grandad James too because you all drilled it into me, and I—" I almost choke on my breath, slamming to a halt and wrapping my arms around my middle as I struggle to get enough air into my lungs. "Oh, God."

Tears stab my eyes, and I'm shaking all over. I can't

do this. How can I do this? I'm only sixteen. My life as I knew it is over. My dreams and everything I thought I had planned is now dust in the wind. I am so screwed. And such an idiot.

Kyler yanks me into an embrace, and I let him. "We have all been sixteen, Hewson. I remember what a confusing time it is. We all fucked up so bad on countless occasions." He holds my face in his hands and eyeballs me. "Trust me when I say there isn't anything we can't deal with. Tell me what's going on, and we'll figure out a way to resolve it."

I bark out a laugh as I shuck out of his hold. "There is no easy way of resolving this." There *is* a way, but it's not something I could ever consider. When it was proposed, it took me all of two seconds to dismiss it outright. No, there is definitely no easy way out of this. "I made this mess, and it'll be up to me to take responsibility for it."

"Take responsibility for what, Hewson?" Kyler asks, the expression on his face strained and serious.

"My girlfriend is pregnant, and she's blackmailing me."

Hewson, a spin-off stand-alone new adult romance is slated to release later in 2022. Subscribe to my newsletter to keep updated with this and other releases. Type this link into your browser: http://eepurl.com/dl4l5v

Want to binge read another series? Check out my *Rydeville Elite Series*, *Sainthood Series*, or *Mazzone Mafia Series*. Exclusively available on Amazon. Free to read in Kindle Unlimited and also available in paperback and audiobook format.

Turn the page to read a sample from **Cruel Intentions**, book one in the *Rydeville Elite Series*.

#1 NEW ADULT & COLLEGE ROMANCE BESTSELLER

In the power struggle between two elite groups, one feisty girl will bring them to their knees…

Life is a cruel game where only the most ruthless survive. It's a truth my mother rebelled against, and she paid for it with her life. Now, I play their game. Publicly accepting the destiny that lies in wait for me when I turn eighteen.

But, behind closed doors, I plot my escape.

Trent, Charlie, and my twin, Drew, rule the hallways of Rydeville High with arrogance and an iron fist. I execute my role perfectly, hating every second, but they never let me forget my place in this world.

Everyone obeys the rules. They have for generations. Because our families have always been in control.

Until Cam, Sawyer, and Jackson show up. Throwing their new money around. Challenging the status quo. Setting hearts racing with their gorgeous faces, hot bodies, and bad boy attitudes.

Battle lines are drawn. Sides are taken. And I'm trapped in the middle, because I made a mistake one fateful night when I gave my V-card to a stranger in a blatant F you to my fiancé.

I thought it was the one thing I owned. A precious memory to carry me through each dark day.

I couldn't have been more wrong.

Because the stranger was Camden Marshall, leader of the new elite and my perpetual tormenter. He hates me with a passion unrivaled, and he won't be the only one. Fire will rain down if the truth is revealed, threatening alliances, and the power struggle will turn vicious.

My life will hang in the balance.

But I'll be ready, and I'm not going down without a fight.

****

Available now in ebook, paperback, and audiobook.

Cruel Intentions Sample – Prologue

Abby

Waves crash against the empty shore, summoning me with invisible arms, and my feet move toward the icy water as if I'm pulled by a string. I'm numb inside. Hollowed out. And I just want to put an end to this... charade that is my so-called life.

I never remember a time in my seventeen years on this earth where I had free will. Where every aspect of my life wasn't controlled and mapped out.

And I'm done.

Done with the mask I've no choice but to wear.

Done with the elite crap I'm forced to participate in.

Done with that monster who calls himself my father.

I want out, and the turbulent sea offers me salvation. I scarcely feel the deathly cold water as it swirls around my ankles like the tempting caress of a destructive lover. My silk robe offers little protection against the bitter wind whipping my long dark hair around my face, and goose bumps prickle my skin in everyplace it's exposed.

I walk farther into the water, my body shivering and shaking as the wild waves lap at my calves. An eerie voice echoes in my mind, urging me to stop.

Imploring me to go back.

Pleading with me not to give up.

Suggesting my world is about to change.

I ignore that taunting voice, tilting my head up, surveying the crescent moon in the dark nighttime sky, casting strangely shaped shadows on the land below. My ears prick at the sound of splashing behind me, and my heart beats faster as adrenaline courses through my veins, but I don't turn around.

"Hey. Are you okay?" a deep masculine voice asks from close by.

I'm standing knee-deep in icy-cold water in the middle of the night in minuscule clothing. Does it fucking look like I'm okay? My snarky alter ego mentally responds to his question, but I remain mute. I can't summon the energy to speak or to care what the stranger thinks of me.

I just want him to go away. To leave me alone. To at least give me this.

But no such luck.

He wades through the water, his darkened form brushing against my arm as he moves around me, positioning himself directly in my line of sight so I've no choice but to look at him.

A flicker of warmth enters my chest as I stare into sultry brown eyes that are so deep they're almost black. The glow from the moon casts a shadow around his form, highlighting his masculine beauty in all its glory. He's wearing low-hanging cotton shorts and nothing else. His bare chest is an impressive work of art that speaks to incredible dedication in the gym. His cut abs are so sharp they look painted on. But it's the tattoos on his chest and lower arms that grab my attention. None of the guys at Rydeville High would dare ink their skin. It wouldn't fit the reputations they've so carefully cultivated or suit their obnoxious parents' plans for their futures. The elite wouldn't dream of lowering themselves to something so provincial.

This guy is an enigma, and the first sparks of curiosity ignite inside me.

My eyes trail up his delectable torso, refocusing on his face. He's watching me carefully. Absorbing my gaze like he wants to bury deep inside me and figure me out. My fingers itch to run along the fine layer of scruff adorning his chin and jawline. To mess up his hair which is styled long on top and shorn close to his skull on both sides. A craving to explore his chiseled cheekbones, and to taste his full lips, hits me out of nowhere, reminding me I'm still very much alive.

I can't ever recall having such a strong, physical reaction to a guy upon sight. None of the guys back home have affected me so potently, except for Trent—he makes my skin crawl with the barest of looks—but this is the complete opposite.

One glance from this stranger heats my blood and

stirs desire low in my belly. I cock my head to the side, intrigued and aroused, my previous self-destructive mission all but forgotten.

We don't speak. We just stare at one another and an electrical current charges the small space between us. My body emerges from its semi-comatose state, and I'm equally hot and cold. A shiver works its way through me, and I wrap my arms around my slim frame, desperately trying to ward off the biting cold air clawing at my pale skin.

"You need to get warm." The stranger extends his hand. "Come with me."

I wrap my hand around his without hesitation, and we tread through the water back toward the shore. His callused palm is firm against my skin, sending a flurry of fiery tingles coasting up and down my arm. We don't speak as we emerge from the sea, walking across the clammy sand toward a small wooden cabin in the near distance. I hadn't noticed it when I first arrived because I had singular focus.

A thin stream of smoke creeps out of a narrow chimney, and I watch the cloudy spirals with fascination as we walk hand in hand toward the neat wooden structure. In the distance, a sprawling mansion occupies prime real estate, the property submerged in darkness at this late hour.

He pushes open the door, stepping aside to allow me to enter first. A blast of heat slaps me in the face from the roaring open fire, and my body relaxes for the first time in days. The cabin is small but cozy and welcoming. The main room contains a compact kitchen with a stove, sink, and a long counter with three stools. On the right is a three-seater couch positioned in front of a coffee table and a wall-mounted TV over the fireplace. A side room suggests a bedroom with en suite bathroom, and that's the extent of the space.

My bedroom is bigger than this entire cabin, but it isn't half as inviting.

A bright rug resting atop the varnished hardwood floor, the soft colorful throw on the couch, and an abundance of vibrant cushions injects a comfortable, lived-in feel. The old bookcase tucked into the corner between the wall and the door is crammed full of books, DVDs, and mementos, creating a homey atmosphere. The only light is from the flickering flames of the fire and an old-fashioned lamp on top of the coffee table.

He shuts the door and steers me in front of the fire. On autopilot, I raise my palms, relishing the heat as it wraps around my chilly skin. He moves around behind me, but I don't turn to look. I stand in front of the fire, allowing it to thaw my frozen limbs and fracture the layer of ice surrounding my heart.

"Sit down," he commands in that rugged voice of his, draping a blanket around my upper body.

I sink to the ground without a word, tucking my knees into my chest as I peer at him. He drops down in front of me, gently uncurling my legs, drawing one into his lap as he dries my damp skin with a soft blue towel. We stare at one another as he dries both my feet and legs, and that same pull from before pulses between us, rendering some invisible connection.

"I feel like I know you from somewhere, yet I've

never seen you before," I admit, eventually finding my voice.

He stalls with his hands on my feet, piercing my gaze with his intense chocolate-colored one. "I know," he says after a few beats.

When he tosses the towel aside, I move closer to him, sitting up on my knees with my body resting on my ankles. I keep my eyes locked on his as I reach up and touch the shorn side of his head, my fingers trailing over the velvety soft hair, tracing the edge of his skull tattoo. It was too dark outside to notice it, but now, I'm even more intrigued by this elusive, hot stranger who appeared out of nowhere to rescue me.

The tattoo is in the shape of a cross, and I wonder if the symbolism means something personal to him. All I know is it's sexy as hell, and my body naturally responds to him, arching in closer.

He pulls my hand away from his head, pressing a feather-light kiss to the sensitive skin on my wrist, and I feel his tender touch all the way to the tips of my toes. His gentle touch is in direct contrast to his edgy look. With his defined abs, bulging biceps, and ink-covered tan skin, he looks like the quintessential bad boy every girl gets warned about. "Why were you out there?" he asks, keeping his gaze locked on mine.

I could lie, but I'm tired of all the lies.

I'm tired of saying what's expected and pretending to be someone I'm not.

"I didn't want to feel anymore."

There's a pregnant pause as he stares at me, no doubt wondering if I meant that sincerely. "What would you have done if I hadn't spotted you?" he inquires, still trying to puzzle me out.

I shrug. "Kept walking most likely." Allowed the sea to claim me as I'd originally intended when I'd given Oscar, my bodyguard, the slip, and driven here.

"Who are you? What's your name?"

I cup his face, deciding on the truth again. "I'm nobody. I'm invisible. I don't exist except to obey their commands."

A slight frown creases his brow. "If you're in trouble. If—"

"Don't." I cut across him. "I don't want to talk about it."

Silence engulfs us for a few beats. "What do you want?" he asks, his voice dropping a notch, sounding wholly seductive, although I'm unsure if that's on purpose or not.

"I want to feel something real," I reply without uncertainty. "I want to let go of these chains that bind my body. To feel like I'm in control even if it's only an illusion." My eyes stay locked on his, and electricity crackles in the air again.

He rakes his gaze up and down the length of my body, his heated stare lingering on my chest as my nipples harden. His eyes flit to my mouth before he licks his lips and drags his gaze upward. His eyes bore into mine, and butterflies scatter in my chest, my heart beating faster and faster as my body heats in a whole new way. "I can help with that."

This time, there's no doubting his intent, and my core

aches with need. My gaze drills into his eyes, projecting my acceptance and permission.

Nodding slowly, he pulls me onto his lap, circling his arms around my waist. "Are you sure?"

I bob my head. "Please make me feel alive. Make me feel like me. Remind me why I should live."

It's crazy.

I don't know him.

He doesn't know me.

But I feel more hopeful in this moment than I have in years.

Slowly, he brings his face to mine, brushing his lips against my mouth. I close my eyes as my body sags in relief. Snaking my arms around his neck, I angle my head as he caresses my mouth with his luscious lips. His kiss is unhurried and worshipful. His mouth moves leisurely and seductively against mine, and this kiss is unlike any I've ever experienced before.

Trent kisses with years of pent-up anger and aggression behind his punishing lips, and it makes me feel dead on the inside. This stranger's tender kisses unravel the knots that usually twist in my gut, breaking through the walls that cage my heart, allowing warmth and pleasure to invade every single part of me.

I meld my lips and my body to his, straddling his hips and gasping as his hard length nudges against the softest part of me. He rocks his hips gently in expert, measured movements, and a burst of desire shoots through me, over-taking logic and warning and common sense.

I shouldn't be doing this here with some guy I don't know.

It would enrage my father, my twin brother, Drew, and my fiancé, Trent, if they saw me, but that thought only spurs me on, strengthening my resolve.

He stands, holding me to him, and I tighten my legs around his waist as he walks toward the bedroom. Our mouths never separate as he lowers me to the bed, and we gradually shed our outer layers.

I've never been naked in front of any guy before. Trent repeatedly tries to strip me bare, but I enjoy denying him. Now, I spread my legs for this beautiful, rugged stranger, with no hint of nerves or vulnerability, admiring his gorgeous body as he pulls a condom out of his bedside table and rolls it over his impressive length.

We don't talk, but words are redundant. He settles between my thighs, bringing his hot mouth to my pussy, and I almost lift off the bed as he devours me with his tongue and his fingers, quickly bringing me over the edge.

No man has ever done that to me before, and the pleasurable sensations coursing through my body are wholly new. When I come down from the best orgasm of my life, he climbs over me, kissing me passionately as his hands caress my small breasts. His roughened fingers tweak my nipples like he's plucking strings on a guitar, rolling them skillfully until they're taut peaks, and it's not long before I'm writhing in need again.

He positions himself at my entrance, stalling to look at me. "Are you sure this is what you want?" he asks, and another little chip melts off the block around my heart.

No one has ever cared to ask me what I need or what I want, and tears prick my eyes at the obvious concern in his eyes.

"Yes. I want to do this with you."

His eyes are glued to mine as he slowly inches inside me. He stops halfway in, sweeping his fingers across my cheek. "You're so beautiful." He nudges in a little more. "And so tight." He flexes his jaw, and I can tell he's exercising caution. When he pushes in a little more, a sharp sting of pain jolts through me, and I wince.

His eyes pop wide as he holds himself still. Shock splays across his face. "You're a virgin?" he splutters.

A sly smirk slips across my mouth. "I was."

"Fuck." He leans down, kissing me so sweetly I feel like crying. "You should've said."

And have you change your mind? Not likely.

Thoughts of losing my virginity to that psycho Trent were part of the reason drawing me to the sea tonight. I've been holding him off for years, but with the wedding approaching, I know I can't hold out much longer.

Denying him that victory only adds to the joy of this moment.

But it's way more than wanting to one-up Trent.

I want to give my body to this gorgeous stranger.

To enjoy this one night where I can take something for myself before returning to the gilded cage I live in.

"It doesn't matter," I say, bucking my hips up in encouragement. "I want this with you. Right here. Right now. Nothing has made so much sense in a long time."

***

Available now from Amazon in ebook, paperback and audiobook format.

About the Author

Siobhan Davis is a USA Today, Wall Street Journal, and Amazon Top 10 bestselling romance author. **Siobhan** writes emotionally intense stories with swoon-worthy romance, complex characters, and tons of unexpected plot twists and turns that will have you flipping the pages beyond bedtime! She has sold over 1.5 million books, and her titles are translated into several languages.

Prior to becoming a full-time writer, Siobhan forged a successful corporate career in human resource management.

She lives in the Garden County of Ireland with her husband and two sons.

You can connect with Siobhan in the following ways:

Website: www.siobhandavis.com
Facebook: AuthorSiobhanDavis
Twitter: @siobhandavis
Instagram: @siobhandavisauthor
Tiktok: @siobhandavisauthor
Email: siobhan@siobhandavis.com

Books by Siobhan Davis

KENNEDY BOYS SERIES

Upper Young Adult/New Adult Contemporary Romance

Finding Kyler

Losing Kyler

Keeping Kyler

The Irish Getaway

Loving Kalvin

Saving Brad

Seducing Kaden

Forgiving Keven

Summer in Nantucket

Releasing Keanu

Adoring Keaton

Reforming Kent

Moonlight in Massachusetts

STAND-ALONES

New Adult Contemporary Romance

Inseparable

Incognito

When Forever Changes

No Feelings Involved

Still Falling for You

Second Chances Box Set

Holding on to Forever

Always Meant to Be

Second Chances Box Set

Reverse Harem Contemporary Romance

Surviving Amber Springs

MAZZONE MAFIA SERIES

Dark Romance

Condemned to Love

Forbidden to Love

Scared to Love

RYDEVILLE ELITE SERIES

Dark High School Romance

Cruel Intentions

Twisted Betrayal

Sweet Retribution

Charlie

Jackson

Sawyer

*The Hate I Feel**

*Drew**

THE SAINTHOOD (BOYS OF LOWELL HIGH)

Dark HS Reverse Harem Romance

Resurrection

Rebellion

Reign

Revere

The Sainthood: The Complete Series

ALL OF ME DUET

Angsty New Adult Romance

Say I'm The One

Let Me Love You

ALINTHIA SERIES

Upper YA/NA Paranormal Romance/Reverse Harem

The Lost Savior

The Secret Heir

The Warrior Princess

The Chosen One

*The Rightful Queen**

TRUE CALLING SERIES

Young Adult Science Fiction/Dystopian Romance

True Calling

Lovestruck

Beyond Reach

Light of a Thousand Stars

Destiny Rising

Short Story Collection

True Calling Series Collection

SAVEN SERIES

Young Adult Science Fiction/Paranormal Romance

Saven Deception

Logan

Saven Disclosure

Saven Denial

Saven Defiance

Axton

Saven Deliverance

Saven: The Complete Series

*Coming 2022

Made in the USA
Columbia, SC
04 April 2022

58488804R00107